ONCE
UPON
A
TIME
IN
HELL

First published 2013 by Solaris
an imprint of Rebellion Publishing Ltd,
Riverside House, Osney Mead,
Oxford, OX2 0ES, UK

www.solarisbooks.com

ISBN: 978 1 78108 155 6

10 9 8 7 6 5 4 3 2 1

A CIP catalogue record for this book is available
from the British Library.

Designed & typeset by Rebellion Publishing

Printed in Denmark

ONCE UPON A TIME IN HELL

BOOK TWO OF THE HEAVEN'S GATE TRILOGY

GUY ADAMS

SOLARIS

To my posse at Solaris,
and Sheriff Jon 'Holy Roller' Oliver
in particular,
for having my back and
keeping me fed with bullets.

1

AT THE END OF
THE RAINBOW

CHAPTER ONE
A LONG RIDE FROM HELL

1.

MY NAME'S PATRICK Irish and I'm a liar.

If you're the sort of reader that requires reassurance that what you're reading is true then it's best you're aware of my pedigree. Of course, if you *are* that sort of reader then God help you, because all writers are liars. It's what we do. Even when we're trying to tell the truth, which I'm doing now.

My career of falsehoods is, perhaps, a little more outrageous than others. I started out with good intentions, something the philosophically-inclined amongst you would be quick to point out is a surefire way of reaching Hell (in that, it has clearly proven successful). I wrote all manner of tales, offered ghosts and ghouls, murderers and spies, monsters and explorers. They weren't terribly good.

Then I found my milieu (forgive me, a posh word, we writers love them). I became the world-renowned

Roderick Quartershaft, explorer, adventurer and figment of a desperate imagination. It is more than possible that you've read some of my stories (according to my gleefully rich publisher there are few in the English-speaking world that haven't, and he has the house to prove it). It is equally possible that you read those stories believing them to be real. The Volcanoes of Hades? The Rat-Men of Sumatra? The Cradle of Life (that outlandish basin in Antarctica that is alleged to contain a jungle so dense and populated as to rival anything along the banks of the Amazon)? Thrilling places, filled from root to canopy with fantastical beasts, wild natives and creatures from myth and history. All dreamed up in a whisky-haze from the comfort of my study in London. I hope admitting as much doesn't lose my publisher that house of his, he's a scurrilous old rogue but he's done well by me over the years. Perhaps those stories will continue to be enjoyed. Perhaps their provenance doesn't matter. Perhaps.

Roderick Quartershaft is dead, that's the important thing. He died on a journey the like of which he had never before imagined. And that it is saying something. In the company of the English inventor Lord Forset and his daughter, Elisabeth; The Order of Ruth, a small brotherhood of monks; and Billy Herbert, engineer and driver of the wondrous Forset Land Carriage (a train with no track, by any other name), Quartershaft faced the like of which his pen had never dreamed. I think that's what killed him, either that or his drinking (which lingers, though I'm trying, dear Lord I am). By the time our party arrived at its destination, this camp, he had expired due to a surfeit of lies. I am the man left behind.

So it falls to me, Patrick Irish, the liar, to tell you some of what came next. To tell you about Wormwood, that impossible town that appeared out of nowhere containing a doorway to the afterlife. To tell you, in fact, what may be the most important and unbelievable story you will ever hear.

It's up to you how much of it you choose to believe, though some of it will now be a matter of history and therefore, one might think, undeniable. Undeniable, that is, if you choose to believe historians any more than you do authors. Which you shouldn't as they're all liars too.

2.

THE CAMP THAT grew in that open plain that might have been Oklahoma, or Oregon, or Ohio (we all traveled our own journeys and yet somehow shared a destination), had grown large by the time Wormwood appeared.

Families, adventurers, outlaws and clerics, our population came from all walks of life, all gathered to wait for the impossible.

Wormwood, it was said, would appear as if from nowhere. It would exist for one full day then vanish again. During that time it would offer a door to what comes after. Be it Heaven or Hell—the difference between them could be said to be subjective—you could walk into the afterlife and take a look.

I was reminded of the hucksters that littered the midways of America's fairgrounds. Sharp-suited and silver-tongued, they promised glimpses of the impossible, a peek at the freakish. Wormwood had a huckster of its own—he called himself Alonzo—but we'll come to him later.

First, let me paint you a picture of that camp because, beyond all the fantasies and horror, this is still a story about the only thing that really matters: people.

During our journey, the passengers on the Forset Land Carriage had assumed, with some arrogance, that we were on a singular quest. A moment's thought should have dispelled that notion. We were composed of three distinct parties: the late Quartershaft, the Forsets and the Order of Ruth, all of whom had heard about Wormwood through their own means before pooling their information and agreeing to travel together (here you can once more see the guiding hand of my publisher, a man that knew a possible best seller when he was presented with the chance of funding it). If we had all heard of Wormwood, why then should we expect others had not? In a world filled with millions upon millions of people, knowledge shared by a few hundred is still tantamount to a secret.

We had narrowly escaped death at the hands of a tribe of Indians, a bizarre, hybrid people with limbs of iron and hearts of coal-fire and hissing pistons. Emerging from a narrow pass through the mountains into this open space, we found we were faced with a burgeoning gathering of folk. In fact, it occurs to me now that, while waiting for one town to appear, another was all but built. Some had been there so long as to construct rough homes, others slept beneath canvas or the stars. Perhaps we should have given the settlement a name. If pressed for a suggestion I would likely have offered 'Hope', but then, I had become a sentimental fool on my 'road to Damascus'.

We were better suited to a comfortable wait than some of our fellow travellers, having sleeping accommodation, a kitchen and stores that extended beyond the simple ingredients most were forced to subsist on. At night, the entire camp would be lit by cooking fires, the air filled with the rich steam of many meals. Often I would walk a winding path amongst them, a trek timed by a decent cigar. The variety on offer never ceased to amaze me. Londoners think they are well-versed in diversity, and yet, in truth, we rarely stray from our defined groups. Here was a microcosm of the very Heaven we aspired to enter—rich and poor, black and white, young and old, the camp was as rich a mixture as the stews they placed on their fires.

I took to documenting the journeys of some of them. I would like to say that I wanted to mark them down for posterity, but perhaps I simply wanted to capture stories. Either way, I'm not sure it matters.

There was the negro nurse, Hope Lane, and her charge 'Soldier Joe', a war veteran who had spent the last few years as an unwilling performer for Obeisance Hicks, a travelling preacher. 'Soldier Joe' suffered from stigmata, making him a superb cash draw for Hicks' crowds. Hicks was now dead, his tame messiah a free man if only he could be unshackled from the chains his own disabilities wrought on him.

And what of the blind shootist Henry Jones? The skin between his nose and hairline was utterly smooth. God, in his perverse wisdom, had decided not to grant the man eyes. Jones had somehow prospered with a gun despite this obvious handicap. From the whispered reports I heard, he had been feared in every town across the country, a wild and dangerous outlaw. But no more, it would seem. His hands ruined by frostbite, he had lost the majority of his companions. Knee High, a dwarf, was the only other surviving member of his gang, one-time performers in Dr Bliss's Karny of Delights (I cannot be blamed for the spelling, not all men were born to wield a pen). The Geek, a savage man who would eat nothing unless it was alive, Toby the Snake Boy and—most painfully for Jones—Harmonium, his wife, had all been lost *en route* to Wormwood.

And of course, perhaps most importantly in the events that were to trigger history, there was Elwyn Wallace, travelling with an aged gunslinger who—according to both Wallace's report and those who slept alongside them— appeared to contain fire in his belly. While sleeping, the old man's mouth, nostrils and even eyes glowed with the light of those internal flames. Elwyn had been travelling to the West coast to take a position in a bank, a simple ambition that he would never attain. Nobody knew the old man's name, nor seemed to consider the fact strange. According to Elwyn, whenever he thought about asking, the voice died in his throat, and he had long-since given up trying.

I could go on, naturally; this place was filled with characters and stories. But there's no need. As well as being liars, writers have one other defining characteristic: they are insufferable know-it-alls. Out of a crowd of characters they can point to a distinct handful and warn you to mind them well. Why? Because they know how the story is to turn out and they already know the key players in what is to come.

3.

AND THEN THE town appeared.

I am tempted to say that there are not words to successfully capture what happened, but that would be an admission of literary mediocrity too far. If I must be a liar and a know-it-all, let me at least take consolation from the fact that I pursued those sins with literary skill.

I hadn't given a great deal of thought as to how the town would manifest itself amongst us. Indeed, when Quartershaft had been behind the wheels of this ageing body of mine, he had considered the whole thing a fool's errand. Once we had completed our journey, that cynicism had gone. I'm not altogether aware of the moment it departed. There was no defining realisation, no sudden conviction. It was something that occurred in hindsight. I found myself sat in one of the chairs we'd positioned outside the Land Transport, looking around at the crowds, aware—with some amusement—that I was as certain of Wormwood as everyone else.

As to the specifics of its appearance, I couldn't predict it. Would it simply arrive, empty space one minute and then a town the next? Would it fall from the sky? Or perhaps push itself up from within the earth itself? (Those last two rather depended on the province of the afterlife I now realize; was it a celestial Heaven or a subterranean Hell?)

In actual fact the process was gentle, a gradual shift in the reality of the plain ahead of us.

It began in the sky, the clouds building as if for a storm, a thick, curdling of cumulus and cirrus that piled high into the clear blue. Then came rain, thick and heavy, purple-tinged, that pounded down on the dust, leaving marks that made it seem as if a stampede of invisible animals had passed.

Then the air seemed to coalesce. I was reminded of the heat mirages I had seen on my journey west, the way the vista in front of you would gain weight, distort as if through a weak lens, as if the air was so affected by the sun it had begin to fry. After ten minutes or so, that distortion began to take tangible shape. A straight line here or there, the hint of a rooftop, a railing, the boardwalk, a doorway.

Small towns over here had fascinated me, the way they were so functionally built from timber. I was used to the weighty permanence of stone or tile, but here everything was erected with hammer, saw and nail. It made the towns seem like toys to me, full-size replicas of doll's houses. I had no doubt that such an attitude was doing a disservice to the hard work of those who had built such homes (I had been known to get confused trying to open a window, let alone construct one). Culturally, though, it was something I had yet to get used to. That said, it somehow made the construction of a town something I was able to relate to. I had no real concept of the use of brick and slate, but I could look at those American conurbations and see them for the man hours they represented, the long days of sweat and splinters. Watching Wormwood materialise was an entirely different experience, an entire town dreamed into life in a matter of an hour or so.

We began to walk the half mile or so towards it, crowds of the expectant moving across the plain in a way that could hardly fail to bring biblical imagery to mind.

As we drew closer, we could hear the town gaining weight, a creaking and groaning of wood as the dream of it became solid and was forced to settle.

A ring of people formed around it, nobody quite daring to cross over the threshold and set foot within its streets.

I had become separated from the rest of my party, rubbing shoulders with strangers as I tried to get a better view.

Wormwood was immaculate, real in everything except an affectation of age. The structures were clean, roofs unstained from winter rain. The signage (Milton's

Supplies, 'Best Value in Town') wore fresh paint, un-faded from the sun. It was an illustrator's impression of a town, an impossible perfection as yet unspoiled from having to exist in the real world.

A bright pulse of light burst from the town's centre. Nobody could recognise its source; from all angles it was obscured, flowing from a building just around the corner from everywhere you could possibly be. The crowd panicked slightly, everyone taking a few steps back, one particularly nervous old maid knocking my notebook from my hands as she made to run for the safety of the camp.

There was nothing to fear. The light faded and all was quiet.

A murmur of fresh excitement worked its way through the gathered hopefuls as a figure appeared at the end of one of the town's streets. He began to walk towards us. I would later discover that this same man had appeared to walk towards every portion of the crowd, a simple miracle by comparison with the manifestation of an entire town, but further, delicious proof of his unearthly provenance.

He was terribly familiar. A blond-haired fellow in a smart suit and waistcoat. The last time I had met him I had been drunk (this was not saying a great deal; I had been drunk a lot of the time). He was the man who had first approached me with regards the myth of Wormwood. He had presented himself as an enthusiastic follower of my work, a devotee of Quartershaft's adventures, with a brilliant idea as to where his next could take place. I began to feel like a character in one of my own fictions (which, now I come to think about, is exactly what I've always been), manipulated to this very spot by the hand of a divine author.

"Welcome!" he shouted, his voice carrying perfectly, either through a natural gift as an orator or, more likely, a magical quality of amplification. "My name is Alonzo. And I'm here to welcome you to Wormwood.

"You've been through terrible ordeals to get here"—there was a general murmur of consensus on this—"and some of you have travelled thousands of miles to reach this point. Well, what can I say? What has come before is nothing. This is where your adventure really begins."

Which, naturally, could only be true: we stood at the threshold of Heaven (or Hell). It would be a terrible anti-climax were the real world—however outlandish it had proven itself to be over the last few days—found to rival its wonders.

That factual point aside, I grew cold at his words. This is not a case of dramatic exaggeration (though I admit I am only too capable of such trickery) rather a genuine sense of unease. There was something, a *quality* to the words, that struck me as not altogether positive. He had the air of the showman, yes, and his speech could have been taken in that context, the theatrical host promising fresh wonders in store. Somehow, however, the words also struck me as a warning.

"Never before," he continued, "have we seen such a response to our arrival. Never have so many undertaken a pilgrimage to our door." He bowed his head as if saddened. "And to think, of all those who perished en route." He smiled. "But then, they made their way to us all the quicker. Death is a road like any other, after all. A painful one at times, certainly, but I hope you'd agree the destination is worth the journey.

"Because there are so many of you, we will need to organise ourselves a little differently. For now I must ask you to wait a little while longer..." There was a predictable uproar at this, to which he raised mollifying hands. "Please don't worry, time is ours to control. You will all get to walk our streets. Just not all at the same time. We will need to take you a party at a time."

Again this caused dissent, but he held up his arms for quiet and got it. After all, as argumentative as the crowd certainly was, it takes a greater confidence than was to be found here to pick a fight with an emissary from God. "Patience. You have waited this long; another hour won't hurt."

And with that, he turned on his heels and walked away again, leaving several hundred people utterly bemused. A couple made to follow before finding that they were unable to pass from the plain into the streets of the town itself. It was as if there were an invisible barrier lying at a defined point between one world and the next. Those attempting to cross it ended up falling back into the dust, embarrassed and angered even further.

The air was filled with questions:

"But it's only supposed to be here for twenty-four hours anyway! We're wasting the precious time we have!"

"Since when did Heaven get so small it couldn't accommodate a crowd of a few hundred people?"

"Maybe they're not going to let us in after all..."

They were all good questions, and many like them passed through my own head. For the most part, though, I was unsurprised. The dominant feeling I had was that of being part of someone else's plan. I had been manipulated to this place and now the plan continued to unfold.

The mistake you are all making, I thought, as I pushed my way through the crowd in search of a familiar face, *is the assumption that you were ever in control of this situation. This was not a cheat. This was not you getting one over on Creation. This was the plan from the beginning, and now we'll see how it plays out. What God wants, He gets.*

Or maybe I'm just being wise after the fact. We writers are terribly prone to that sort of thing.

4.

I HAD BEEN hoping to find the rest of my party, but the familiar faces I stumbled upon first were those belonging to Elwyn Wallace and his aged companion.

"Well," he said, "I won't lie, I was hoping for more than that."

"You'll get it," said the old man, staring over my shoulder at Wormwood.

I told them my thoughts, my suspicion that all of this was pre-ordained and part of a bigger plan. The old man said nothing, but gave a small nod. Trying to talk to him was as productive as discourse with a rock. He looked like one too. A particularly ugly piece of granite that had been left in too many rainstorms.

"I guess God moves in mysterious ways, huh?" said Elwyn.

The old man gave a gruff laugh at that. It sounded like an engine driver shovelling coal.

"Well," the young man continued, ignoring his friend, "I didn't even know I was coming here, so what do I care if I have to wait another hour?"

* * *

5.

I FOUND ELISABETH Forset and Billy shortly after. They had moved away from the main crowd, sitting down on some rocks a little distance away.

"Welcome to Heaven," said Billy. "Join the line and wait to be seen. Who knew the afterlife would be like visiting the dentist?"

"I hope it works out to be a little less painful," I replied, sitting down next to them. "Did you recognise Alonzo?"

"Nope," said Billy, looking to Elisabeth, "you?"

"Never seen him before," she replied.

"When I was a child," I said, "my grandfather built me a puppet theatre. It was the most wonderful thing. Florid proscenium arch, real velvet curtains. Beautiful. The puppets were designed after Punch." I looked to Billy. "Do you have Punch and Judy over here?"

"Never heard of it."

"It's a puppet show about a psychotic wife beater who kills his baby."

"Sounds charming."

"In our country we think of it as a comedy for children."

"Now I understand why we decided to go it alone."

"The puppets were all hand carved, strung on wires, and I would sit and play with them for hours, making up my own stories. That's probably where my love of stories came from. It was my most favoured possession. Until, like all children, I suddenly forgot about it and it was left to get tangled and jaded. But for those few months there was nothing I liked more than making them all dance to my stories. God to those little, clacking people."

Elisabeth smiled. "And now you know what they felt like?"

"Absolutely," I nodded. "I wonder how your father's feeling? I can't imagine he's one for sitting quietly and waiting his turn."

"The last I saw he was storming off in the direction of the Land Carriage, muttering. He'll be back soon, I'm sure."

"He'll probably try and drive the thing through the town," said Billy, "smash his way into the ever-after."

"You think you're joking," Elisabeth sighed.

"What about our brotherhood?" I asked. "I imagine they're probably happily praying their appreciation heavenwards?"

Elisabeth nodded towards the rear of the crowd where I could see them doing just that.

"If they get an answer," Billy wondered, "maybe they'll be good enough to pass it on."

"You're being frightfully dismissive of a God that's probably sat a few yards away," noted Elisabeth, her voice perfectly serious. "I wonder if that's a good idea."

"If God is as all-powerful as I've been led to believe," said Billy, "He'll hear me clearly whether I'm sat here or in Tucson. Proximity ain't got a thing to do with it. Besides, I don't mean any harm. I'd hope He can take a joke."

"We'll find out soon enough," I said. "That's a rather worrying thought isn't it? As long as God is speculative—or, at the very least, insubstantial—He's open to interpretation. He can be the wise beneficence Jesus spoke of or the terrifying brute that commanded Abraham to kill his son as a test of his faith. Who knows what He's really like?"

"I hadn't thought about it," Elisabeth admitted, "until now."

We looked towards the town and waited for our strings to be tugged once more.

*   *   *

6.

"IT'S JUST PREPOSTEROUS," announced Lord Forset, who had indeed returned, albeit sans Land Carriage. While this was a relief, it might have allowed him to more easily bear the burden of the supplies he had brought: notebooks, tools, an Eastman Kodak box camera, a food hamper and a rifle.

"Planning on shooting a cherub?" Billy asked, noting the rifle.

"In my current mood I wouldn't rule anything out," Forset replied. "Everything I've ever read about Wormwood contradicts this farce of a situation. Organised walking tours of the afterlife? Ludicrous and utterly contrary to the principles of scientific exploration."

"You don't know it's going to be quite that bad," Elisabeth said, hoping to reassure him.

"No? Look at it. Like a crowd loitering outside the zoo, waiting for the ticket office to open. It won't do, it won't do at all."

He sat down on one of the rocks and proceeded to mop at his face with his handkerchief. "When the town appeared in the Cotswolds, it was as a delicate miracle. Fading out of nowhere to the surprise of the locals, who were able to cautiously explore it before it vanished once more. This? Look at it. It's a massive spectacle, a theatrical nonsense put on for the pleasure of the gathered hordes."

"You don't know for sure whether the Cotswolds appearance is even true," his daughter pointed out. "You only have one man's report to go on, after all."

"My very point! Hardly going to happen this time, is it? There will be shelves of books written on the subject by the time this lot have finished."

"And you'll probably have written one of them," I pointed out, choosing not to mention that I would certainly be the author of another.

"What does it matter?" asked Elisabeth. "Is a miracle only worth exploring in isolation? So it's not as well-guarded a secret as you expected..."

I couldn't help but make the observation I mentioned earlier, that even this many people were the merest drop in the ocean when one considered the population as a whole.

"I know, I know," Forset agreed. "It's foolish and selfish of me. I've been imagining this moment for most of my life. The fact that it isn't how I imagined it is hardly a surprise; it's just going to take me a while to get used to it, that's all."

7.

WE WAITED TOGETHER for another twenty minutes or so, until, finally, there was sign of life once more from within Wormwood.

That bright light that had acted as a theatrical cue for the enigmatic Alonzo pulsed from deep within the buildings. From this slight distance it looked like the detonation of an explosive charge.

The crowds had dissipated slightly. Like our party, they had separated out into their little groups to discuss and moan about the unforeseen state of affairs. Now they consolidated once more, swelling towards the borders of the town.

Alonzo's voice carried through the still, afternoon air, clear even at the back of the crowd.

"Thank you for your patience," he said, "it is with pleasure that we welcome the first of you to pass beyond the gate and into what lies beyond. Before you travel I must try and prepare you for what you are about to experience. It is a mistake to view the existence beyond this as a singular, definitive space. It can be that, but it is also much more. At its most extreme, it is a subjective environment, a place coloured by the soul of the one who enters. I cannot, therefore promise that all who enter will be glad they did so. We will talk again soon."

The mood of the crowd changed again, from impatience to fear. Not that it did anyone the least bit of good. No puppet-master allows his creations choice, after all.

The entrance to Wormwood was not to be taken on foot. One moment I was stood there in the real world and the next...

I was somewhere else entirely.

INTERLUDE ONE
HATRED OF GOD

1.

THE RESPONSE FROM the crowd was predictably slow. Everyone was busy staring at Wormwood, groups breaking up, people jumbled in the crowds like several packs of playing cards cast into the air and then left to scatter. Eventually, enough people had begun looking around, trying to find friends and family who were no longer there, that the penny dropped.

"They've just vanished," said Billy, looking to Forset and his daughter, "including Patrick... just lifted out of the air and pulled into the town."

"I'm sure they're alright," said Elisabeth, "nothing bad can have happened to them."

"You know that, do you? I don't have the same faith in that place as you."

She took his arm. "I'm not sure I have any faith in it at all, but panicking isn't going to help."

He nodded.

All around them people were talking, shouting, praying. Some treating it as a glorious miracle, others as a heart-breaking slur. Billy noted the Order of Ruth, moving in a solemn procession towards them.

"Well," he said, "of all the people I would have expected to have been amongst the first called."

Father Martin offered a rather insipid smile. "Perhaps we can do more good out here than we can there. God has a plan for us, I'm sure."

"For all of us, perhaps."

"Certainly."

Father Martin took this as affirmation, but Elisabeth was aware Billy hadn't meant it as such. "And how are you, Father?" she asked, shifting the subject slightly. "It must be a wonderful feeling to be so close to God?"

"We are always close," he replied, taking her hand. "He lives in everything and everyone. Though I'll admit it does my spirits good to see so many uplifted by the miracles we have witnessed."

"Uplifted?" asked Billy, "personally I just feel scared."

"I'm sure there's no need for fear," the monk replied. "It can be difficult to let go of what we have always believed—the rules of science, the firm earth beneath our feet—but this is the work of God, and God is good."

"Well, that's as may be, but I still don't like not knowing what's happening to those people. Patrick is our friend, he's been through a lot..."

"His own road to Damascus. Yes, I believe I even heard him refer to it as such."

Billy shrugged. He gave up on discussing it. Father Martin was perfectly entitled to his beliefs, but at that point they ran so contrary to his own that he couldn't see the point in continuing the discussion.

He was saved the need to try. From the far side of the camp a scream rose up, tearing its way across the plain.

"Great," he said, breaking into a run. "More trouble."

2.

THE MAJORITY OF the camp had emptied as Wormwood had appeared, but a few had stayed, including Jeremy Clarke, the man who had found himself the sole doctor in the assembly.

"But we've come so far!" his wife had said, tugging his arm.

"It's not going anywhere just yet," he had replied, "and I'd hardly be worthy of stepping across its threshold if I left these people to die in my absence. You go along, I'll be with you as soon as I can."

The couple had dreams of being reunited with Jack, their son, who had fallen from the roof of their house five years earlier. If you had asked him during their long journey to Wormwood if there was anything more important to him than seeing Jack again, he would have offered you a sad smile and a shake of the head. It had been the one thing that had pulled them along the trail. He would have told you that nothing, *nobody*, was as important to him as that. But now, when faced with the choice of abandoning those who needed him, he found he couldn't do it.

The road to Wormwood had been hard for everybody, but some had survived it better than others. In his care he had a handful of people who he was by no means sure had survived it at all. The fact that they still drew breath held little sway with him. "You just check and see if they're breathing tomorrow," he would have told you. "Then we'll know if it killed them or not."

Up until last night, he would have said one of the most likely contenders for that deferred death would have been the blind man, Henry Jones. He had suffered from exposure and frostbite, his hands a ruin of blood and rot. He had been a dangerous man, so some had told him when he had been recognised (a man with such a distinctive appearance could hardly remain anonymous for long). Clarke would not have classed him as dangerous any longer. Though Jones had fought even that pre-conception, waking in the early hours and fighting anyone who tried to hold him down, determined as he was to leave the tent and search for his absent wife, a woman Clarke could only assume had not been so lucky as her husband. Or indeed, the rest of the man's party, a wounded war veteran, his negro nurse and a dwarf—as absurd a band of folks as Clarke had ever found in his surgery. Finally, he had quietened the man, injecting him with a brew of tranquilizers that allowed all concerned some much needed peace and sleep.

Jones aside, Clarke had an elderly woman who had not been fit for the journey her family had brought her on; a combination of exhaustion and a pre-existing respiratory condition had put her next on his list of 'Fatalities that Just Don't Know it Yet'. Along with a kid whose broken leg had turned septic on the trail, his fever now so high Clarke gave him no more than a few hours.

So how could he have abandoned them? Even if his care made no difference in the end, even if they died despite his best efforts, he would fight to do his job. It was who he was.

A few hours ago, the nurse, Hope Lane, had woken up and he'd found her in a surprisingly stable condition. So much so that, as the day wore on, she showed an almost full recovery. He would have been tempted to call it a miracle had that word had any viable currency left. He roped her in to assist him and, while she was still a little sluggish and dehydrated, she had seemed more comfortable being part of the solution than the problem.

Once they had been left almost entirely alone, the rest of the residents, his wife included, walking across the open land towards the town, she truly proved indispensable. It had been left to the two of them to tend to the sick.

"Why has my Joe not woken up yet?" she'd asked him, brushing the limp hair back from her charge's forehead.

He didn't like to admit that he hadn't expected either of them to recover, particularly as she had proven him at least half wrong already, so he simply patted her on the shoulder and turned her attention towards another patient. "He'll wake when he's ready," he'd told her, "and not a moment before."

And so they had continued to work. They paused briefly as the words of Alonzo had carried even as far as the camp, impossibly clear, as if he stood within the tent itself. While the response amongst the gathered crowds bordered on the hostile, Clarke was actually relieved at the delay. It meant that he hadn't missed the chance to see his son just yet. Given time, he could see to his duties and also pay Wormwood a visit. Perhaps it would be possible for the nurse to cover for him, she certainly seemed capable.

This was not to be as, twenty minutes later, she vanished, alongside Soldier Joe and the troublesome Henry Jones.

* * *

3.

WHEN BILLY REACHED the all but empty camp, he had little difficulty finding the source of the screaming. A girl of no more than twelve was hunkered down behind a rock at the far reaches of the camp, where it met the incline of the mountains behind it.

"Mama told us we had to wait," she said, "had to be clean before we set foot before the eyes of the Lord."

A small crowd had gathered at Billy's back now, all drawn by the sound. He looked up to see Clarke, the doctor.

"What's happened?" the man asked.

"Damned if I know," Billy admitted. He looked to the girl. "And where is your mama now, sweetheart?"

The girl pointed towards the slope behind them. Now he looked carefully, Billy noticed a thin red line working its way along a trail between the rocks.

The girl sobbed. "The Devil took her!"

2

HELLBENDERS

CHAPTER TWO
THE GODLESS ONES

1.

"COME HERE," THE old gunslinger said, "you and I need to talk."

Given his usual reluctance to do any such thing, this was encouragement enough for me to perk up my ears and listen. The look on his face was as miserable as a pig on the butcher's block but, hell, weren't it always? I decided I shouldn't pay too much heed to that unless what he had to say gave me due cause. Besides, as stupid as it'll sound, I'm sure, I was growing bored out there in the crowds. Bored, you say? Damn you, Elywn, what kind of idiot are you that you could lose interest when presented with a magically appearing town and the voice of the Almighty (if, indeed that's who it was; I am not a man of ecclesiastical leanings—after all the things I've seen, even less so—but when someone's talking to you from the gates of Heaven, I am inclined to assume that if it ain't God Himself it's someone who knows Him on a personal level). Well, I am inclined to the opinion that boredom is the essential human condition and any situation, once experienced for long enough, can bring on a solid bout of it. Yes, Wormwood had appeared out of nowhere, but it had then proceeded to sit there doing sweet fuck little ever since. There was only so long you could stand next to a complete stranger, roll your eyes and say "Woo-ee, that town sure wasn't there before, huh?" before both of you go your separate ways and wonder when something new is going to happen. Most of the crowd was doing the same thing, shuffling back in the general direction of camp. After all, if we were just going to be vanished into the place when our time was due, there weren't no need to kick our heels on its doorstep; we might as well get some coffee on the go and put our feet up. The old man, however, had a more active plan for the evening ahead.

"We need to get in there," he said. We'd made our way up into slightly higher ground and were sat looking down on the open plain, now a bottleneck stoppered by the town that had appeared at the mouth of the mountains ranging to either side.

"We will," I replied, "soon enough."

"No," he said, "we go in there under our own steam. That is, if you're willing."

I shrugged. "I'm willing, I guess. You've kept me alive this long."

He looked slightly awkward at that, by which I mean his blank expression twitched ever so slightly, like a horse fly bouncing off a tombstone. He wasn't what you would call expressive.

"I wish I could tell you," he said. "Being here, seeing the games and manipulation. I don't like it. Wish I could be better than that..."

"But there are some things you just can't tell me," I said, "I remember. 'Laws that cannot be broken.'"

He nodded. "Partly that. Partly because to talk of things is to invite being overheard."

"I don't think anyone's going to hear what we're saying up here."

"No?" He nodded towards the town. "The person I'm thinking of can hear pretty much whatever they want."

He took the time to think for a moment. "I'll be as honest as I can be: accompanying me will be dangerous, terrifying and horrible. But I can't do it without you."

"I guess I should be grateful you're asking rather than telling."

He shrugged. "I'm not going to force you."

I thought about it, but not for long. I trust it's already perfectly clear that I'm not what you would call a brave man. I have been known to cower in thunderstorms and cross the road to avoid big dogs. Still, I wasn't someone who was used to being needed, either. That, and the fact that, for all his faults, the old man had played fair by me so far, made my mind up.

"I'll come."

He nodded. "Thank you. Then we wait for it to grow dark and we make our move."

"Dark? Will it make it any easier to hide from..."

"Don't say the name."

"Fine... 'Him'... if it's dark."

"No. But He's not what I'm trying to hide from in the first instance. We don't want the rest of these folks to know what we're doing either."

"You think they'd try and stop us?"

"I think we'd draw too much attention, that's all. And I don't like attention."

*   *   *

2.

WAITING FOR THE dark wasn't so bad. That time of the year, the sun fell low pretty early, and it was only a matter of a couple of hours or so before we were on our way. We left our animals tied up by our belongings, trusting that if there was one place you should be able to leave your belongings unattended it was on God's doorstep, and waited in the rocks above Wormwood.

By this point most people had returned to the camp. Once it was clear that their sticking close to the town didn't offer any advantage, the draw of a warm blanket and food cooking on a fire pulled all but the most devout from their vigil. The few that were left were the kind of folks that would likely never move again. I had seen one of them a few times around the camp, a wild-eyed man with tattoos of Bible verses etched all over his skin. Some of us had taken to calling him King James, being the witty sons of bitches we were. He stayed out there on the empty patch of land between the camp and the town, muttering his prayers and waving devout arms skyward. It occurred to me that even now, with the doorway to Heaven right in front of him, he couldn't help but address his prayers to the sky. Habits break hard.

We stuck to the higher ground, meaning to move around the back of Wormwood if we could, so that the town would block the view of us from the camp. Not that it was likely they'd see us anyway. The sky was cloudy and the moonlight as thin and rare as water in the desert. Several times I stumbled as we made our way through the rocks, the old man turning and giving me the sort of look you give a small child who will keep insisting on pouring his food all over the table.

"You may have eyes like a rabbit," I whispered, "but us mortals find running through rocks at night to be a tricky business."

We descended on the far side of the town where the coast was, as far as we could tell, clear. If there were any extra zealots lurking in the darkness, we'd have to hope that their minds were on their prayers, not whoever else might be running around out here.

"So," I asked, "how you figuring on getting in? As far as I could tell earlier the whole place was sewn up as tight as a saloon-owner's purse. It looked like the streets were wide open, but if anyone tried to walk on them they ended up flat on their ass in the dirt."

"It's just a door," he said, "and any door can be opened with the right key."

He snapped a piece of branch from some low scrub and held it up to his mouth. That terrible light bloomed in his throat and for a moment his mouth was full of fire. He breathed on the wood and it smouldered in the heat. Then he rubbed at the glowing end with his thumb.

"You ever had a cough?" I asked him, "I imagine you could kill a man if you came down with a head cold."

He didn't reply, just stood up close and began to draw on my forehead with the singed end of the branch. Not the most common response I'd gotten to one of my jokes, but less violent than some.

"There," he said, having scribbled some form of swirling pattern on my skin, "we have a key."

"Right, whatever you say. You need me to do you?"

He shook his head and threw away the branch. "I can come and go as I like, as long as I'm with you."

"Yeah, 'cos I'm real important like that."

"You are now."

He led me by the arm to one of the open streets, the faint light falling down through the row of perfect buildings.

"You might feel dizzy as you cross the threshold," he warned. "Pay it no mind, the feeling will pass."

We stepped forward and, though there was no sign of a barrier between us and the street ahead, it felt as though I was passing through a cobweb made of molasses. The air pulled at me, my skin tingled and, as predicted, my head exploded like a firework, bright lights flashing in front of my eyes and my legs cutting out from underneath me. If it weren't for the old man I would have ended up flat on my back, but he stopped my fall and dragged me over towards the boardwalk, where I sat down and waited to get my balance back.

"My head is burning," I said, once I got my voice back.

I reached for my forehead, where he had drawn the mark, but he pulled my hand away. "Don't," he said, "the burning will pass and you need the protection a little longer."

"Protection," I managed to repeat before turning round and chucking up my guts into the dust at my feet. When it comes to being sacrilegious, I won't have it said I do things by halves.

After a couple of minutes I was feeling well enough to move. I got to my feet and began to stagger along the street. "If this is Heaven, I can't say I'm much impressed."

"This is just the way station," he said, "The Transition. This is the first step on your way to the afterlife, and it's designed to be familiar. That's why it always fits in wherever it manifests itself."

He pulled me to one side as a small twister worked its way along the street, kicking up dust as it passed.

"A shade," he said. "A soul that has yet to cross over."

We worked our way along the street and I was reminded of Wentworth Falls, the living town that had nearly done for me a few days earlier. It had that same false air to it. A town where everything had been built yesterday and nobody had got around to living in it yet. Some of the buildings had shop signs, others were just homes; a short distance ahead was what looked like a saloon. As we approached, a faint light began to trickle out from beneath its swing doors, getting brighter the closer we got.

"That where we're going?" I asked.

He nodded.

I stood still outside the saloon, the light now so bright that I had to hold my hand up in front of my eyes to cut down on the glare. I turned to face him, pointing at my head. "The key going to come in handy again?" I asked.

"That and the soul you've got inside you."

"It ain't going to take that off me, is it?" Not that I'd been using it much.

He shook his head. "But if you haven't got one, then you need to be travelling close with someone who has."

I followed his meaning. "You lacking a soul? I thought everyone had one."

"Not of my kind. It was one of His gifts to you. If you can call it a gift..."

"Can't say I've had much call to use it. Don't even know what it's for."

"It fills a hole."

He took my arm and led me up the steps and through the swing doors. The light filled my vision and I couldn't see a thing in front of me. I just kept walking, hoping I wasn't going to crash into anything.

"This going to..."

3.

I HAD BEEN going to ask whether passing through the light was likely to make me feel sick again, but the question was redundant after my stomach answered it.

As the light surrounded me I felt the floor vanish beneath my feet. There was the brief sensation of floating and then the ground was back. Except now I was lying on it and my head felt like it was being chewed on by dogs. I was having a great time.

I tried to look around, but it felt like I was still stuck inside the light, a burning kick to the eyes that had me screwing them shut and pressing my hands to my face.

"Wait," came the old man's voice. "It takes a moment."

What takes a moment? I wanted to ask, but the pain in my head was so all-consuming I couldn't be bothered to speak. It was something that could only bring more pain and didn't seem worth the effort.

Then, all of a sudden, the light ceased. It showed how much effect keeping my eyes shut had had; the minute it was gone I felt the difference. The pain in my head went with it and I finally opened my eyes.

I was lying in a valley, mountain ranges to either side. The rock was dark and sharp, the sort of thing you'd cut yourself open on if you tried to climb it.

"This is Sheol," the old man said, walking into my line of sight. "The second stage. It always takes a moment to solidify. The Transition is real but it reflects the mind of those who cross it. It feeds off your head, trying to temper itself in a way you can understand."

"This is all out of my head? I'm imagining it?"

"It's real enough. Just subjective. It needs to calibrate to your wavelength."

He was talking more than usual, shame I couldn't understand a word of it.

"You know what a metaphor is?" he asked.

"Of course." I didn't. "I'm not stupid."

"This is like that. Something big and complicated expressed in a way that allows you to understand it."

"It's not doing a great job." I sat up, feeling the dust beneath me. "It's like ash."

"Old bones," he said. "Try not to think about it."

Too late for that. I brushed my hands on my shirt and stood up.

The valley stretched to either side for longer than my eyes could see. A constant corridor.

"Is this where the others came?" I asked. "The ones who were vanished up first?"

"No, we're going the long way round. They will move directly through the Transition to their final destination. We're entering the place physically, and that takes boot leather and strength."

"Good." I tried to shake the dust from my shirt. "Really good."

"It's hard to sneak in through the front door."

"I guess. How long a way round? This place looks like it goes on for miles."

"It does. We're going to need to find ourselves something

43

to ride." He squatted down in the earth, digging away at the dust with his fingers.

"We going to hitch a ride on some worms?"

He pulled a long bone out of the ground, then another, and another...

"You planning on building something here?"

"Actually, yes." He held up what looked like the skull of a large deer, two large horns stabbing straight out from what had once been the top of its head. "All I need is enough of it for the rest to..."

Before he'd finished speaking the ground began to ripple and move as more bones pulled themselves free of the dirt and into the air.

The old man kept digging, unearthing another skull. This one had the look of a giant ram, it's head just as big as that of a horse but with the distinctive curled horns on either side. He threw it to the ground a short distance away from the other bones, which were still moving, pulling themselves together and clicking into each other.

After a minute or so, there were the complete skeletons of two creatures stood before us, the deer and the ram, swaying slightly on dry joints.

"Everything clings to life," he said, "here more than anywhere. It remembers what it once was."

"So I'm dreaming them as well?"

"You're not dreaming anything. I told you. You're..." —he struggled for the words—"translating a little, that's all."

"Given a choice, I'd have translated that pair of ugly bastards into something with a bit more meat on it."

"Just climb on, let's get moving."

"Climb on?" I circled the ram, not able to believe the thing was ever going to take my weight, certainly not without splitting me in half ass-upwards. I watched as he pulled himself onto the deer, grabbing hold of its bones as if it were a ladder and dragging himself onto its creaking back.

"Fuck diddly," I moaned and did the same, the ram's bones holding fast as I tugged at them.

Finally I was sat on it, both hands gripping its spinal column tightly for fear I'd fall off.

He gave me one last, lingering look. For a man whose face didn't move much it sure seemed to offer its fair share of opinion. He seemed to go from sympathy to contempt without so much as moving a muscle. Maybe I imagined it.

"Let's ride," he said, kicking at the hollow flank of his beast.

I'd thought my old mule was bad. At least he'd had the odd ounce of fat and a saddle to lessen the beating on your buttocks. For those wishing to recreate my journey, might I suggest they strip naked, squat and then proceed to firmly beat their gaping asshole with a stick. Do that for an hour or so, just long enough that you've scared that poor puckering bastard into never opening again, and you've about got the measure of it.

The view didn't change for some while, enough that I began to wonder if we weren't just riding in a circle, a wide trench coiled around our destination. The hooves of the old man's dead ride kicked up clouds of ash that I had to ride through, desperately trying to think of it as nothing more than dust.

Every now and then I got a sense of movement on either side of us: nothing I could ever focus on but enough for me to know that we weren't alone in that place, however empty it might seem at first glance. I did my best to pay it no mind. If something planned on leaping down on us, then my companion had already proven himself handy in a fight. I'd more than likely be able to practice my special skill—running like hell—while he did something violent. He wouldn't mind, he was used to me by now.

After about an hour there came sign of something ahead, a large gateway built into rock the same dark shade as the escarpments either side. The gate was of old wood, scorched and warped. Above the gate were what I first took to be statues, and then, as we drew closer, sentries. They were like no other beings I had seen, each sat quite comfortably on a separate chair that overlooked the causeway and the door that offered escape from it.

On the left was a creature that reminded me of some of the pictures of Injuns in feathered headdresses I'd seen when I was a kid. At first I took it to be wearing a heavy coat of black raven feathers but, once I was close enough to see clearly, I could tell the feathers were its own. They shimmered and rustled, undulating as if things worked their way between them, giant fleas perhaps. Which left me to wonder if fleas would feed on one of their own, because the legs that protruded from the feathers were definitely those of an insect, thin and segmented, the joints hooked and vicious. It's head showed the same split origin, a sharp, pointed beak jutting out from beneath big, segmented eyes like those of a fly.

Next to him was the most human of the trio: a woman whose skin fluttered around her in dried flakes. A creature of dust. She wore a waistcoat that I took for leather until I spotted the pert nipples to either side of its thin lapels and was forced to accept that the skin had been flayed from a man rather than beast.

Finally, the least definable of the three. It was a figure lacking dimension. As it turned you were presented with a rough silhouette, like a child's drawing of a man, then it would turn again and it was lost from sight as you were presented with the thin edge of the paper. It was a sketch brought to life.

"And who do we have here?" asked the woman in the centre. "What little man is this who wishes access to the Dominion of Circles?"

They were looking at me, and, having hoped that the old man would do all the talking, I looked to him for advice. He simply held his finger up to his lips, like a child asking you not to rat out its behaviour to a vindictive parent. He slid from his skeletal ride and immediately began to climb the escarpment to the left, the three gatekeepers not acknowledging him one bit.

"Well?" squawked the bird creature. "Cat got your tongue?"

"I would like its tongue," the woman said. "I would wear it like a tie."

"Maybe I'll roll the dice with you for it," said the bird, "as I bet it would make a nice snack too. A fat, spurting worm that would lick all the way down the gullet. A French kiss that fills the belly."

The third creature, the insubstantial impression of a man, fluttered and I saw words appear above its silhouetted head like smoke signals, melting away the moment they were read.

Flesh suit, the words said. *Precious warmth. Wear it till it melt.*

"I think its damaged," said the bird. "It cannot speak. Its brain has curdled. Maybe it's a Buzz freak. You like Buzz, little man?"

"Mmmm..." The woman licked her dry lips, pink clouds of lip skin fluttering in front of her yellow teeth like butterflies as her tongue dislodged them from where they nested on her skull. "Curdled brains served hot from the skull like oatmeal, perhaps we could share?"

She reached for the bird creature, her skin thrown into temporary disarray as she moved, revealing the skeleton beneath. When she was still once more, her hand resting on her companion's feathered shoulder, the skin settled, dressing her once again. "A romantic meal," she continued, "to sharpen all appetites."

The bird-thing turned to her, its beak chattering in what I took to be pleasure. "My appetite is always sharp."

Sharp, appeared in a word cloud above the third creature's head. *Brittle. Cut. Shine.*

"I think I'd prefer my brains to stay exactly where they are," I said.

"It does speak!" The woman clapped her hands into swirling clouds of dust.

Speak, appeared above the third's head, then: *Scream*.

"I'd rather not do any screaming just now," I said. "It's been a hot ride and my throat's parched. Maybe after a rest and a nice cold drink I could work up a holler or two, but not right now."

I couldn't say where this sudden reservoir of fortitude sprang from; most likely the fact that, out of the corner of my eye, I was watching the old man creep closer and closer to where the three beasts were sitting. Why they couldn't see him was beyond me, but clearly they couldn't, and equally clearly, he had a plan. It seemed the best way forward just to keep chatting until he got around to acting on it. Besides, my throat *was* parched...

"It's a cheeky little thing!" said the bird. "I can't decide if I like it or hate it."

Hate, suggested the third, the word swelling slightly for emphasis before it broke up.

"We could always play with it for a little while," the woman suggested, "just to decide if it's entertaining."

"What would we play?" the bird wondered. "Bleed the Pig?"

"Split and Spit!" said the woman, laughing so hard her own skin vibrated all around her so she appeared little more than a blur.

Skin the Dog? wondered the third, the word 'dog' briefly running through the air above its head.

"I don't suppose the three of you could be persuaded to start off with a little poker first, and see how things move on from there?" I asked.

Strip, offered the third, though I was fairly sure he would want me to take off more than just my undershirt.

"How did you come to be here, little thing?" asked the woman. "I can't smell the grave on you."

"Perhaps the earth was particularly sweet," suggested the bird. "You don't get here with a heart that still pumps, after all."

The picture of a beating heart appeared above the third's head.

"I may have got turned around a little. I was aiming for California."

"California is not a dominion I've heard of," said the bird. "Perhaps it's one of the new settlements. They say there are camps springing up all the time on the shores of the Bristle."

"Maybe he's one of Greaser's people," suggested the woman. "His popularity is on the rise, so the whispers tell me."

Whispers, agreed the third. *Soul farts*.

The old man had made it to the top of the gate and was now walking along behind their chairs. Still they seemed to have no idea he was there. He pulled out his gun and pointed it at the head of the bird creature.

"The kid's with me," he said and pulled the trigger.

There was a startled squawk and the air filled with feathers and brains.

The old man kicked the woman's chair forward, and she fell with a yell of surprise. When she hit the ground, she exploded in a cloud of dead skin. The skeleton at the heart of her broke into separate pieces, but immediately rolled around trying to reconnect.

"The skull!" he shouted. "Grab the bitch's skull!"

This was not a suggestion I took kindly to, but the urgency of his words and the innate trust I'd developed for him had me running towards her thrashing bones before I really had time to question the sense of it.

Her skin was whipping around like a swarm of flies wanting nothing more than to calm down and settle back down on a nice piece of shit.

I grabbed hold of her skull, avoiding the gnashing teeth.

"Throw it up into the air," he said, "high as you can."

I did so, sending it sailing up above my head. A pair of eyes appeared from within the cloud of skin, clearly hoping to bed themselves back down in their sockets. They were too late. The gunslinger took his shot and blew the skull into fragments. The eyes dropped back down to earth like gelatinous hail stones.

"What about that?" I asked, pointing to the third, who was flexing in what could have been anger or panic. It presented itself as a series of static images, like a magic lantern show. Flickering silhouettes, some more human than others. A man throwing his hands in the air, a large wolf's head roaring, what looked like flames...

"Yes," the old man asked, "what about you? Are you going to try and fight?"

It swept towards him with the sound of a blanket being whipped in the air before seeming to vanish inside the gunslinger. For a few moments the old man looked troubled, as if stricken by gas after a heavy meal, then that flaming light in his throat sparked once and he exhaled a slow plume of deep, black smoke.

"The Consequence is a conceptual creature," he said. "Its power lies in corrupting the mind with its thoughts and ideas."

"And you're beyond corruption?"

"Hardly that. But I'm certainly out of its league."

He began to climb back down the slope, his boot heels kicking up twin waves of ash as he slid towards ground level.

"Who were they?" I asked.

"Lesser presences," he replied. "Gatekeepers, loiterers, gossipers. Nothing worth talking about."

"Oh, good," I said, "as long as they weren't terrifying or anything."

"Terror is more than an ugly face," he said, reaching the bottom. "There are things ahead that will make them seem like the pale shadows they were."

"You say it as if that's reassuring. It's not."

"Just saying it like it is."

He walked up to the gate and threw his weight into pushing it wide open. "Appreciate a hand here," he said.

"Fine," I stood next to him. "I just get to forgetting you can't do everything by yourself."

"If I could you wouldn't be here, boy."

Slowly the gate parted, the two heavy doors swinging to either side. The ash clouds this kicked up forced me to close my mouth and eyes as I kept pushing.

"Can't see a damned thing," I said, waving my hand in front of my face.

A cool wind hit my face and, as the ash settled, I found the world had changed.

"Welcome to the Dominion of Circles," he said.

INTERLUDE TWO
IN THE NAME OF THE FATHER

1.

To DESCRIBE THE movement between outside and in is quite impossible as there simply didn't appear to be any.

One moment I had been walking towards the town and then the next I was within its streets. I looked around, assuming that I would see Alonzo, or one of the many other people I assumed had been brought within Wormwood alongside me. There was no sign of anyone. I was, as far as I could tell, quite alone.

At a loss as to an alternative plan, I decided to explore.

I crossed the street to peer into one of the shops, stopping almost instantly to investigate the dirt at my feet. It would be disingenuous of me to suggest I had given the ground any thought but, if pressed, I would have assumed it to be the same patch of empty earth that had been sitting here minding its own business before someone dropped a magical town upon it. Taking a handful of the dry, powdery stuff that shifted beneath my boots, I realised that couldn't possibly be the case. It had the texture of ash; the remains of winter fires or funeral pyres. It was entirely different from the heavy, clay-laden soil we had been tramping across for the last few days, dirt that would have swallowed us all had any heavy rains come. Perhaps it wasn't important, but it made me think nonetheless. How much of this town was physically real? Was it a solid chunk of matter—extending down even into the earth foundations—brought from elsewhere? Was it just a dream of a town? (If so, then had they had gone so far as to dream the dirt I walked in?) Was it somewhere else entirely, a place that appeared to exist right before us and yet really was simply a representation of another place entirely? Had the dirt changed because I was now many miles away from where I had last stood?

Surrounded by miracles, you might wonder at my obsessing over such detail, but I was determined to know the answers to this place, inside and out. Naivety? Yes. Of course. I would be shown to be an idiot for believing such things to be within my comprehension soon enough.

I mounted the boardwalk, unnaturally aware of the feel of the wood beneath me, the physical creak of the planks as they bore my weight. If they were imaginary planks they had been hewn from very sturdy imaginary trees.

The shop that faced me claimed to offer livery supplies. A faux saddle, carved from wood and painted a gleeful shade of red, hung from a chain above me alongside the sign: M. Peele, Livery and Leather Goods.

I looked through the window at the racks of bridles and straps. The wall was festooned with them, pulled from one hook to another until the whole resembled nothing less absurd than a web as spun by a cow. There was no sign of a shopkeeper, so I pushed open the door and stepped inside. The air was heavy with the smell of leather. Everywhere you looked, studs and clasps winked in the sunlight that passed through the window, every shadow lit by a constellation of false stars.

I pulled at a few, becoming more and more confused as I tried to imagine them applied to anything so mundane as a horse. Following the pattern of the straps and hoops, I had to concede that Mr Peele catered for a wider zoological range than normal. Some—the least bizarre of them—seemed to be designed to harness a human.

The opposite wall housed saddles and here, again, the absent craftsman had refused to be bound by a single species. Some were more than an arm's length, their padding thick and their girth wider than any horse's back. The horns that rose from their pommels were extended and grotesque: military applications, perhaps, designed to intimidate opposing cavalry.

Conceding that Mr Peele was clearly not at home for business, I left his emporium and made my way further up the street.

I glanced in the windows of each building and store as I passed, taking notes, even making the odd sketch.

The only other life I found were the coiling forms of impossibly large silk worms that wove the stock of Ma Ninny's Dresswear & Lace.

Ahead I saw the doors of a saloon; if there were to be life anywhere, I reasoned, it would be there.

There was no sound coming from beyond those doors— not the refrain of a piano, the susurration of conversation, nor even the chink of glass against glass. Nonetheless, I pushed the swinging doors aside and entered the Holy Ass Saloon.

Inside was as empty as everywhere else.

Now, I have sworn to you that I am making the best possible effort to curtail my drinking, and that is certainly true. Liquor was the fuel that kept Roderick Quartershaft running, and I was quite determined that his engine should stay quiet forever more. That said, the overwhelming thirst that struck me as I ran my eye along the bottles behind the bar, like the prizes on a fairground stall, all shining and precious, was hard to ignore. It seemed to me that one small measure, as an aid to fortitude in my current, unusual circumstances, could hardly be seen as a sin.

For all my attempts to convince myself otherwise, it certainly felt like one, as I cautiously made my way behind the bar and gave the bottles a closer examination.

Then my eyes fell on a bottle of Dufrockies Single Malt and my indecision vanished. I simply couldn't resist a taste of it. I had never seen another bottle outside the holiday villa of my publisher, a draughty little pile of bricks and resentful servants he keeps on the banks of Loch Ness. He had bought it locally and we had wrung it dry with increasingly warm enthusiasm. The idea of finding a bottle here should, perhaps, have been no surprise. Whether this was my Heaven or my Hell, both regions could hardly be complete without one. I found a glass and poured a small measure into it. Then topped it up a little. If I was only going to have one—and I was determined that would be so—then let it be worth having. It is the breaking of the resolution that's the thing, not the degree by which one has broken it.

I put the bottle back on the shelf, stood the glass on the bar and stared at it for awhile. It was quite, quite beautiful, the brown liquid glistening in the glass like the most precious stone a man could ever set eyes on. This was my Koh-i-Noor. The perfection I would chip away at, sip by precious sip, never finding the true beauty I thought had lived at its centre. I wanted to drink it very badly indeed but, in the end, I managed to resist. I would like to say that it was simply a case of resolve, but I was also aware of where I was standing. Who could say what other eyes might be watching my deliberation? Was this entire scenario a test? An alcoholic trap designed to judge me?

For all that I wanted that drink, I decided the risks of taking it were too great.

I didn't pour it away. I just left it there like a votive candle, flickering a malty prayer.

I moved back towards the doors of the saloon and suddenly felt my legs crumple beneath me. For a moment I truly regretted not taking that last drink as a bright light flooded over me and I felt myself pass out.

2.

WHEN I CAME to again, it was to the smell of old books. As scents go, it is certainly one that has clung to me over the years. When I was a child, I can remember no greater comfort than to lie on the floor of the library, close my eyes and imagine that smell transmuting to other odours: a summer's field, an Arabian bazaar, an ancient battlefield. Books were the gateway to all these places and countless more. They were my passage outside of myself before the whisky took over the job.

"Mr Quartershaft?" asked a voice. "Or is it Irish?"

"Irish," I replied, sitting up and looking around.

The room was an exact replica of that childhood library. I looked around half-expecting to see the young me curled up in a corner somewhere lost in the fantasies of Sir Walter Scott.

At one end was the walnut desk at which my father would sit and compose his correspondence. If he ever simply sat and read books in the library I had never witnessed it; it had been a place of business not pleasure. Sat at the desk now was Alonzo, looking perfectly at home.

"I hope you don't mind?" he said, gesturing to a book on the desk. "But you were unconscious for some time." He held up the book, *The Water Babies* by Charles Kingsley. "Jolly fun, especially in his open-minded attitudes towards belief."

"'No one has a right to say that no water babies exist,'" I quoted, "'till they have seen no water babies existing, which is quite a different thing, mind, from not seeing water babies.'"

"Quite." He smiled. "Do you, as it were, believe in water babies? You certainly used to; your books were filled with creatures every bit as bizarre and unlikely."

"My imagination has never found it hard to fly."

"Indeed not. More importantly, you have convinced others, have you not? It's all very well to talk of strange tribes and lizard creatures, but making the reader quite convinced they exist? That is another skill entirely."

"You're most kind."

"I am merely stating fact, you are one of the greatest liars of your day."

"I prefer 'novelist'."

He laughed. "The term is interchangeable."

I suspect you know my opinion on that and will therefore hardly be surprised to hear that I didn't argue. Instead I asked a question that had been on my mind for some little time:

"Why did you want me to come here? It seems to me that you made a concerted effort to ensure I did so. Are there a shortage of liars in Heaven? Presuming, of course you don't come from Hell."

"The line can get blurred between the two, though they are two different dominions. To answer your question, the simplest one at least: there are plenty of liars in both. But I wanted one who was mortal."

"I am still that, then?" I asked, "It had occurred to me that I may no longer lay claim to the condition."

"Oh, no. That's one of the rules of the Fastening: you are a visitor, your life is still your own."

"The Fastening?"

"This period, when we join with you, when the barrier between us is lowered."

"Albeit subjectively."

"Ah..." He shifted in his seat, a piece of theatre, I decided, there was no way this man had been truly uncomfortable in his life. "I confess we are being a little more selective than some might hope."

"So not everyone is going to get their chance to see the hereafter?" I smiled. "There certainly are liars in Heaven, then."

He looked at me in silence for a moment, his fingers drumming gently on the surface of his book. "To answer your other question," he said finally and, I noted, ignoring my potential insult, "I wanted you to come here because I have need of your skills."

"Really?"

"Yes, I want you to write a book. A sequel, I suppose you could call it, to a book that we feel has outlived its usefulness. Tell me, have you read the Bible?"

CHAPTER THREE
RED SUN

THE GATE OPENED out onto a large boardwalk and jetty, protruding into a lake so huge we might as well hang it all and just call the damn thing a sea. The air was cooler than before, and the sky was the heavy red of an overripe plum. The water of the lake was dark and thick, surrounded on all sides by mountains that reached up into that miserable looking sky. The shoreline was flat, sown thick with long grasses.

There was a small kiosk at one end of the jetty. A gas lamp hung off the corner of its lopsided roof, throwing a sickly, purple light in a puddle all around it. Here and there other people paced up and down, waiting for whatever boat it was that travelled these waters. Some were clearly human, others less so. I tried not to stare at a thing that looked like a crab with a horse's head, in case it got it in mind to snip my legs off with its pincers.

"The Dominion of Circles?" I asked.

The old man nodded. "Or Hell, if you prefer."

"I most certainly do not. I kind of had my heart set on Heaven."

"All in good time. Our journey must start here."

"And what a lovely place to start."

"It's known as the Bristle," the old man said, pointing at the water.

"Nice name."

"Look at the banks of the lake," he replied. Following his finger I realised that what I had taken as long grass was in fact thick hair. It was as if we had been reduced to the size of mosquitoes, crawling around in the thick beard of a dead man, his mouth wide open and filled with molasses. It was not the most charming place I had ever visited.

"You'll have to buy a ticket," he said. "They can see you."

"But not you? Like the three of them back there? They had no idea you were creeping up on them, did they?"

"I am Non Grata in these parts. Nobody sees me or hears me."

"One of the reasons you needed company, I suppose?"

He nodded. "Now go and buy your ticket."

"Where shall I say I'm heading?"

"There's only one destination."

"How much is it? I left my money belt back at the camp."

"You don't pay with money."

"Shit-fire! I'm not going to like this, am I?"

He shrugged and moved to the edge of the boardwalk to look out over the thick water.

Figuring I had little choice in the matter, I walked up to the kiosk. On the other side of the dirty glass sat a small man in a striped vest. A cap covered his head, strands of white hair creeping out from beneath its tweed. As I drew closer, he looked up at me, his eyes turned into giant, goggling spheres by the thick lenses of his spectacles.

"I'd like a ticket," I said, "for the... you know..."

He just nodded and pulled a stubby piece of card from a small drawer in front of him.

"What do you have to pay with?" he asked.

"How much does it cost?"

He stared at me for a moment, though whether he was suspicious of me or just trying to decide what price he could get away with I couldn't tell.

"I need something precious," he said. "Something you cherish."

I thought for a moment, putting my hands in my pockets. "My watch?" I suggested.

"Time isn't precious," he said as I pulled it out of my vest pocket. "We have all we need of it down here."

I looked at the watch's face, where the hands where moving around seemingly at random.

"What would you suggest?"

"You married?"

"Nope."

"Ever been in love?"

I thought about that. "I guess I've thought so, though nothing that ever stuck."

"What about the first girl you kissed?"

This line of questioning was getting a mite more personal than I had expected from my experience of travelling on ticketed transport.

"What about her?"

"You have kissed a girl, then? Or boy? Whichever floats your boat. We don't give a donkey's dick which way you swing here."

"A girl," I said, quickly, trying not to seem too defensive.

"She got a name?"

"Course she does. Esme Heap."

"I hope she looked prettier than she sounds."

I pictured her, remembering that hot afternoon behind the schoolhouse. I'd been following the trail of a snake, it's curved lines carved into the dusty floor like a child's drawing of the sea. I'd almost bumped right into her, not paying attention to where I was walking. She had been a few years older than me, cocky and sly. She always wore the kind of smile that made me nervous. It was the kind of smile I expected to see on something that wanted to take a bite out of me.

"If it ain't little Elwyn," she'd said, laughing a little and flicking up the hem of her skirts as if about to start dancing. "The quiet one. I like the quiet ones. They're full of secrets."

My first thought was to try and think of one I could offer her. "Rattlesnakes don't have ears," I told her. "They can tell when something's coming by, feeling the ground move." I stamped my foot a little as if to prove the point.

"Well," she said, laughing loudly, "there's a thing to know."

I'd been encouraged by that, so much so in fact that I'd sat down next to her and told her everything I could remember about snakes. Looking back on it, she must have thought I was the most boring kid in the world. Maybe that's why she kissed me, to shut me up. It worked. I was in shock as her face suddenly loomed at me, not really knowing what to do as she planted her lips on mine. Then her tongue pushed its way into my mouth and I thought of snakes again, tasting the air. I made to reciprocate but she'd already pulled back. "That's your prize for being a clever boy," she'd said, getting up and rustling her skirts again. "If you think of any better secrets I'll find you an even better prize." She gave me that scary smile again and ran off. I never dared talk to her again. I wanted the prizes she had to offer, but was scared that I wouldn't know what to do with them when I got them.

"She was pretty enough," I told the man in the kiosk.

He nodded and gave me a smile that reminded me of her. I wondered if he wanted to know anything about snakes.

"It's a nice memory?" he asked. "When you think about it do you get that mixture of excitement and discomfort? Regret but pleasure?"

I'd never thought about it that deeply but, now he'd come to mention it, I told him he was about right.

"Then that'll do."

He handed the ticket over.

"Oh, right then. Thanks."

I took the ticket and looked at it. In fancy writing, it announced that I was entitled to passage on the Riverboat Clearsight.

"When's it due?" I asked, looking back up at him. He'd removed his cap to expose a ruptured cranium, like the split dome of an egg.

He scratched at the wet wound then looked at his hand, idly rubbing the dampness between his index and forefinger. "Who can ever tell? It shouldn't be long."

I decided not to comment on his exploration of his skull, just took my ticket and walked back over to where the old man was leaning against the boardwalk railings.

"Wasn't that difficult, was it?" he said.

"No, he just wanted to know about a girl I used to know when I was a kid."

"Yes? What was special about her?"

I thought about that. "Couldn't tell you. I don't think I ever even talked to her."

He smiled. "It'll come back to you. A boat ticket is cheap, the payment doesn't last long."

I had no idea what he was talking about at the time, so just put the ticket in my pocket and looked out at the water. It was too dark to be able to see it clearly, it just looked like a thick black mass; there was the occasional slopping sound as something moved within it.

"What is it?" I asked. "It sure ain't water."

"You don't want to know. Boat's coming."

I looked up to see the huge shape of a paddle steamer cutting its way towards us. I was sure it hadn't been there before, but that was no surprise; there was no point in expecting the expected here. The black smoke from its funnel pulled a fat line across the red sky, its paddles shining slightly in the pale light.

As it got closer, the crowd on the boardwalk began to gather at the mouth of the jetty, pushing and shoving to be the first allowed onboard. The thing that was somewhere between a horse and a crab did its best to jostle against the crowds, but someone fetched it a solid kick and it toppled off the jetty and into the water below.

"Rather you than me," I said, leaning over to watch as it fought to stay afloat in the thick liquid. Suddenly a pair of hands reached out from the water and latched onto it, pulling it down as it whinnied in fright.

"There's people in the water," I said.

"Ahuh," he agreed, "hungry people. But it ain't water."

As the paddleboat slowed to draw up alongside the jetty, there was a dull cracking sound like lightning and

I looked up to see a flash of white light in the sky. From this bright point a human figure appeared, tumbling through the crimson clouds and falling into the lake.

"Where's he come from?" I asked.

"The lake is filled with souls who feel they deserve it," he said. "That's what keeps it so deep."

As the boat drew to a halt I noticed the blades of the paddle. They were sharp metal, stained with the gore they cut their way through. I looked over the side again and began to realise what it was we were planning on sailing on. 'It ain't water,' he'd said, and I now imagined the thousands of bodies, reduced to thick liquid by the paddles as they cut and chopped on their journey.

"That's disgusting," I said. "What did they do to deserve that?"

"Nobody forces you to be part of the Bristle," said a voice from next to me, no doubt assuming I had been talking to them, my companion unseen. "You wish yourself into the slopping tides, nobody does it for you." I looked to see who was speaking. It had a woman's voice, but the scabbed face that peered out from within its cream-coloured hood could have belonged to either gender. "People are their own worst enemies, aren't they? Begging to have their sins wiped clean with whip or blade or fire. Get over it, you were a shit head, that's what I say."

She smiled and her face cracked. I nodded and gestured for her to step onboard the boat ahead of me.

The man from the kiosk had come out of his booth to be joined by a couple of sailors from the boat. One was a normal-looking man but for the length of his black beard, which he tucked in his belt, and the other glowed with the sort of pale green light you see on night insects.

They lowered the gangplank and began ushering people aboard, the man from the kiosk taking back the tickets he had only recently handed out and slipping them into his pocket.

"Careful who you talk to," said the old man. "Most of them won't pay you any mind, but you shouldn't trust the people you meet here."

I nodded.

"We have a little business to conduct onboard, but stick by me and I'll keep you on the straight and narrow."

I handed back my ticket, suddenly remembering the time I'd kissed Esme Heap behind the schoolhouse, and climbed onboard the Riverboat Clearlight.

INTERLUDE THREE
ONE MORE TO HELL

"THE DEVIL TOOK her," the girl had said, and none of those gathered could summon the confidence to contradict her.

Billy turned to see that Elisabeth and her father had caught up with him.

"Someone should look after the girl," he said to her.

She smiled, though it was false, a pretty thing hung over a trap. "Indeed they should, but don't expect me to do it just because I'm a woman."

He sighed. "I didn't mean nothing by it."

"Of course you didn't." It was clear she didn't believe him.

Clarke had squatted down in front of the girl, taking her flapping hands and squeezing them in his own. "It's alright, child. You just calm down, we'll find your mama for you."

Billy went over to examine the rocks, Elisabeth at his side.

"Blood," he whispered, looking at the thin red trail.

"Mama didn't go quietly."

"What did the Devil look like, my dear?" Lord Forset asked the child.

"Red," she said, "all over his face."

"But he was a man?" the Lord qualified. "He looked like a man, yes?"

She nodded. "But he was the Devil, I know it."

Billy turned to Lord Forset. "Can I borrow your rifle, sir? I'd feel more comfortable if I were armed."

"I'll come with you," said the peer.

"I'd rather you stayed here. No offence, but I'll move quicker on my own."

Forset considered for a moment, then handed the rifle over. "Now is not the time to argue; a woman's life is at stake."

"Thank you." Billy checked the rifle was loaded and accepted extra cartridges from Forset. "I'll do my best," he said to the crying girl.

He was halfway up the rough track between the rocks when he noticed Elisabeth was following. "I said I'd move quicker on my own."

"Haven't slowed you down so far, and as my father said, now is not the time to argue. Keep moving, I'm coming with you whether you like it or not."

Billy cursed under his breath but did as he was told.

He slung the rifle across his back so that he could use his hands to pull himself up through the rocks. The blood trail was fairly consistent, not so heavy as to suggest a fatal wound but steady enough to give him cause to doubt for the woman's longevity. Whatever—or rather, whoever; he wasn't about to believe this was the work of the Devil just yet—had taken her was dragging her behind them as they climbed.

"Whoever it is possesses a good deal of strength," he said to Elisabeth. "It's a fairly easy climb, but not if you're dragging a woman behind you all the way."

He looked further up the mountain, hoping to catch a glimpse of their quarry. The light was beginning to fail now, as evening gave in to night, and the terrain was uneven, the trail winding through narrows all the way. The attacker had more than enough cover to keep them from view.

"You think he knows we're following?" asked Elisabeth.

"You'd think he'd guess it likely. The kid's scream could be heard for miles. Of course people were going to come running."

"I would have expected him to dump the woman and run."

"Yeah, makes you wonder what it is he wants her for."

"Maybe he knows them? It could be something personal."

"Kid didn't recognise him."

He waved at her to be quiet, stopping and listening for a moment. There was a scrabbling sound followed by a slow clatter of rocks.

"He's not too far ahead," said Billy, picking up the pace, almost running up the trail, leaping from rock to rock.

Elisabeth, much to her irritation, struggled to keep up with him. If she had had the good sense to wear a pair of trousers, she cursed, she'd be more than a match for him. She resolved to get changed on their return.

"Stay back," said Billy as she emerged onto a small plateau. He was stood a few feet ahead of her, his voice low and quiet. "You don't need to see this."

Whether she 'needed' to or not didn't matter one damn to Elisabeth, who ignored his advice and stepped up alongside him.

The little girl's mother was lying on the face down on the rocks before them.

"Did she fall?" Elisabeth wondered, noting the spreading pool of blood, quite black in the twilight, that surrounded the body. "Or maybe he dropped her?"

She moved closer, but Billy put his hand on her arm. She shook it off. "Please, Billy," she said, "you're terribly nice, but if you keep insisting on attempts at gallantry we're going to fall out."

She turned over the body and it fell on its back with a sound like wet clothes being beaten against stone.

"She wasn't dropped," she said. "Rocks don't do that much damage."

Billy squatted on the other side. He looked down, suddenly realising he was treading in the woman's blood, then realised there was little he could do about it. The pool had spread so far he could hardly not.

"Like an animal attack," he said, thinking back to the stories he's heard of an engine driver that had worked for the company. The man had left his cab to clear the carcass of a deer from the tracks ahead. As he had been pulling at the animal, he had been set upon by wolves. His engineer had scared the animals away with his rifle but not soon enough to save the driver's life. By the engineer's account—and it was a story he drank on for years—there had been little left of the driver but a pair of legs and some teeth.

He looked around them, unslinging the rifle in case something was bearing down on them.

"Up there," whispered Elisabeth, pointing to a distant silhouette of a man leaping across a narrow crevice further up the mountain. The figure appeared only for a moment, caught against the faint light left in the sky, and was then gone.

"He can't have done this," Billy said. "Nothing human could have done."

"'The Devil took her?'"

Billy couldn't think of a reply.

CHAPTER FOUR
ACE HIGH

1.

THE BOAT WAS the biggest I'd ever set foot on. Three decks, crammed full of passengers of all persuasions. The place rang out with the sound of a calliope, hurling its cheery melody into the air as if it revelled in the sickness that surrounded it. No doubt it did; certainly my squeamishness was noticeably unusual amongst the other passengers, who drank and caroused their way from deck to deck, cabin to cabin.

We aimed for the bar and I was sorely tempted to break the habit of a lifetime and take a drink. The old man had me order a bottle anyway, so that he could partake. The bar staff all wore the same fixed smile—which sounds like one of those literary terms, but I'm no Patrick Irish, I mean it literally: the smiles were fixed with hooks and nails, gaping lips yanked apart to reveal their teeth. I guess the owner took his customer service seriously. I did my best to ignore them, turning instead towards the stage, which was filled with dancing girls cavorting in so lewd a manner I couldn't take my eyes off them (while also being struck by a paralysing embarrassment; I was, you'll remember, something of an innocent back then). The troupe high-kicked to the piped dance numbers, revealing their naked undercarriages to the eager whooping of the front row. My attention was caught in particular by a brunette left of centre. She was quite simply the most beautiful woman I'd ever set eyes on. Her hair in tight tresses, her eyes wild, she danced with such enthusiasm I was utterly swept away by her. The innocent boy inside me did his best to focus on her face, as if he were somehow insulting her to do likewise. He didn't always manage. I'd seen a hypnotist routine on stage once, a crusty old German with a pointy beard striking people brainless with the power of his 'magical mesmerism', leading them around as mindless puppets. He could have saved himself the effort; even at that young age I knew the surest way of making a man forget himself was to put a pair of jiggling titties in front of him. It reduces even the most intelligent specimen to the likes of a panting dog.

"Caught your eye, has she?" the old man asked.

"Who?" I blustered, doing my best to feign innocence.

He took another mouthful of his drink. "You watch yourself, boy; a woman like that is sure to eat you alive."

I shrugged in pretended indifference and went back to watching and dreaming my sordid little thoughts.

"It's a woman we're looking for," he said, "but you won't find her up there. If you can tear your eyes away, she's likely to be on one of the gaming tables."

I pretended I was only too happy to leave, sparing one last glance towards the stage, where I swore the girl tipped me a wink.

2.

WHILE THE BAR had been a raucous and carefree place, the casino took things more seriously. Not that it was quiet: the room was huge, containing somewhere in the region of thirty or forty gaming tables. The call of bets, the spin of roulette wheels and the riffling of cards made a wall of sound that rivalled the calliope and cheering next door. The atmosphere was wholly different though; for all that there was the occasional cheer of celebration, most in the room wore masks of intense concentration, fear and anger. This was a place where fortunes were lost more than won.

I moved past a large woman, bulging in a dress of red satin that made her look like something a butcher had just removed from a carcass.

"My luck's going to turn," she said. "Just you see, any minute now my luck's going to turn."

She closed her eyes and muttered prayers to whichever god might offer her best odds and the wheel was spun. I glanced past her, wanting to see if her prayer was answered. The wheel looked like a living thing, built from cured meat and bone, the ball that bounced between its divisions like a bullet reverberating around a rib cage. It fell into black twenty-two, and she crumpled in despair.

"God damn the thing," she sighed. "Maybe next time... yes, maybe next time..." She began to shake, like she was having some kind of fit, and then slowly toppled to one side. The crowd parted, and she fell crashing to the floor, still quivering as she lay there.

"What's wrong with her?" I asked, but the old man grabbed my arm and pulled me away.

"Don't interfere with the house business. Or we'll never get out of here."

"Shouldn't someone fetch a doctor or something?"

"She's in Hell, boy. What exactly do you think a doctor's going to be able to do for her?"

Yes, well, there was that.

"Just keep your mouth shut," the old man said, "or you're going to draw attention. Remember, you look like you're talking to yourself, nobody can see me."

"Lucky them," I muttered.

"We're here to see a woman called Agrat."

"Pretty name."

"Stop your damned talking." He actually kicked me slightly in the back of the legs as I moved ahead of him. The old man had a temper on him, and no mistake.

"She will be dominating one of the card tables," he continued. "She can never resist a game of chance, and like all the first family, she's powerful enough to win."

I looked around. A thin creature, its arms and legs jointed the wrong way, like those of an insect, turned its single eye towards me and grimaced.

"Just passing through," I said, tapping the brim of my hat. It extended a flat tongue, like a thick slice of ham, and slapped the side of its face with it. Whether this was an insult or just personal hygiene it was impossible to say.

I nearly stepped on another member of the clientele as it slithered its way between the tables, an albino worm that had at least gone to the trouble of putting on a collar and tie. Say what you like about the residents of Hell, they know how to dress. Or not, I was forced to concede, when presented with the dangling pecker of a horned fellow as he turned towards me. I think I must have gasped (the damn thing was dragging its tip on the carpet; as dicks went, it was pretty damn startling). Its owner smiled, apparently pleased to cause such a response. I tried to smile back, but that was made difficult by the fact that the pecker rose up independently and nodded at me.

"Good evening," it said, in a voice of thin, expelled air, "best of luck at the tables."

"Oh, you too," I said.

The penis somehow managed to look gracious as it bowed and then turned away, tapping a woman on the shoulder so that it and its following owner could get past.

"Over there," said the old man, pointing towards the far corner, where I could just about glimpse a tall, brightly-coloured headdress.

Agrat gave the appearance of being a woman in her fifties. She was beautiful, having the sort of pale, gentle radiance you see on old paintings and soap adverts. Beauty that doesn't have to work at it. Her headdress was built from several layers of silk, varying hues of blue and red. When she laughed, as she did often, it rustled as if caught by a gentle breeze, exposing light blonde hair beneath. She wore a dress that made her look even more like royalty, the fabric seeming to change colour as she moved. Everything she did gave the impression of both power and humility, the sort of person who could burn down your house and you'd find yourself thanking them for it. Terrifying grace. I'd all but fallen in love for the second time that evening.

"You need to join her game," the old man said.

"But I'm no good at cards," I said, trying to keep my mouth as still as possible, no doubt offering up a terrible, false grimace.

"You won't have to be. Just do exactly as I tell you and say what I tell you to say. I'll do all the hard work, you just get to translate."

"And whose money they going to take when I lose?"

"I told you before, nobody's interested in money here. We need what she can offer, and the only way we'll be able to get it is if we win it from her. Agrat gives nothing away unless she really has to. Let's get some chips."

"Without money?"

"What can money buy you in Hell? The thing people value here is experience, life lived. Like the ticket seller who took a memory from you for a while. Remember, everyone here is either dead or were never truly alive in the first place: demons, conceptual entities and the such. The more intense the experience, the more valuable it is. You can either loan those experiences to people, like the ticket seller—that's a low cost transaction—or you can give them away permanently, which is much more valuable. The buyer gets to savour that experience again and again for as long as they own it."

"So I need to convert my experiences to chips? What sort of experiences?"

"Anything and everything, the most potent memories you have. Just remember that if you lose them, they're gone forever. Negative feelings can be valuable, as long as they are rich and unusual. Where we are, pleasure comes in many forms. Sometimes there's nothing a low-level punishment demon savours more than being able to experience the fear and pain he dishes out on others. That said, the highest price will always go to the positive emotions, as they're easily exchanged and sold on. Who wouldn't enjoy the sensation of true love? Or an amazing meal? Or a rich and satisfying night of sex? The most valuable thing of all is what we call Package Memories, the entire response to a person. The feeling of love and security for a parent, the love for a husband or wife. But if you lose that, every memory of that person is gone forever. It's a large price to pay."

"I guess they're only memories."

"But memories and experience are what make us who we are. If we were a blank slate every day, what scope would we have to measure pain or pleasure? Life is relative."

We had arrived at a kiosk on the far side of the room. Inside, narrow eyes shaded by a pale green visor, a young woman counted and stacked chips, setting them in neat rows in the racks in front of her.

"What do you have to offer?" she asked.

"Repeat what I say," said the old man, "A life well lived."

"A life well lived." I repeated. The woman nodded at what was clearly nothing more than a formality.

"Give me your hand then," she said and I poked it through the hole in the glass of the kiosk.

"Just the surface," the old man said, "I don't intend to play all night." Then he nodded towards her, signalling me to repeat his words, which I duly did.

The woman chuckled. "A shy one, is it? The old ones soon lose their inhibitions. What do I care for the sticky little secrets, eh? The times you wished someone dead, the dirty little thoughts you conjured up when playing with yourself, the loves never spoken aloud? It's all just dollars and cents to me, honey."

She took my hand and closed those piggy little eyes of hers. After a moment she shivered slightly and a thin strand of saliva crept out of the corner of her mouth. I was about to snatch my hand back in case she went and dribbled on it, when, all of a sudden, a dizziness washed over me and I had to grab on to the side of the kiosk to stop myself falling over.

"You'll be alright," said the old man, carefully standing behind me to offer a little support. "Just go with it."

Images flashed through my head, so fast I was barely able to register most of them. Faces of people I'd known, moments in my life. Some were recent: running from giant beetles or the living streets of Wentforth Falls. Others were older: the face of my father in his cups, or the look of sorrow on my mother's face as I told her I planned to travel. I even glimpsed the face of the dancer next door, the momentary love affair that existed in my mind only, maybe it was worth a few cents...

Finally she let go and the dizziness lifted.

"Well," she said, "I've known richer. I'll give you a stake of eleven dollars. You'll get your memories back when you cash up."

She handed over the chips and, for a moment, I didn't know what I was supposed to do with them. I felt in a daze, so much of my life stripped away and stored in the vaults here at a riverboat casino in Hell. I was half the man I had been when I came in.

"First time?" she asked, seeing I was struggling. I nodded.

"It'll take you a minute while your brain patches over the gaps. You should remember all the important, recent stuff, any friends you came in here with. All it takes is for you to interact with them a little and the memories fall back in place. Now get out of here, you're holding up the line."

I looked behind me and noticed there were now a couple of other people waiting to do business.

"Thank you," I said, and stepped to one side, bumping into an old man who had been standing too close.

"Sorry," I said, "bit unsteady on my feet."

"Take a minute, son," he said. "I'll come back to you."

I looked at him and his face fell into place. "Oh, yes, it's all your fault in the first place. Ain't going to forget you in a hurry, am I?"

"Imagine not." He pulled me to one side. "Now try and also remember that nobody else can see me, then you'll figure why it is people are looking at you funny."

I looked to my left and saw a little girl, maybe eight or nine, dressed in the prettiest little silk dress. She was staring at me in utter confusion. My heart nearly broke to see her in a place like this. Kids died, sure, it was a fact of life, but you hoped they would find themselves in better circumstances than a riverboat floating on the minced up bodies of the dead.

"Hey, little lady," I said, "don't mind me. What's a pretty little thing like you doing here?"

"Choke on my hot shit, whore-master," she replied, and walked off.

"Did you..." I was shaking my head in shock.

"She's no more a little kid than I'm an old fart," he said. "You're going to have to get used to not taking everything at face value. Now let's go and find you a seat at Agrat's table."

I pocketed my chips and followed him back to the far corner, where the game of five card stud was coming to the end of a betting round.

"So what is it we're after?" I asked. "Just so I know..."

"Agrat's power is in incantations. We need her to practise one on me."

A hairy-faced beast was clearly losing what little he had left. He looked like a poster I'd once seen for a dog-faced boy at a carnival sideshow, every part of his body covered in thick, greying hair.

"I'm about cleaned out," he admitted, tugging nervously at the hair on his left temple. "I'll go all in."

"That's wonderfully sporting of you," said Agrat, offering him a smile that looked as valuable as the pot. She offered her cards: a flush that spit all over his triple eights. "I hope you one day get to win some of your life back. I'm sure it was very interesting."

"Mainly people kicking me up the ass, I imagine," he said, "if this last half hour's been anything to go by."

He stood up and the old man pushed me towards his empty chair. "Remember to repeat what I say," he reminded me. "Tell her you want to take his place."

"Right... erm... Any objection to my sitting in?"

The table looked up at me as if noting a passing buzzard that had just taken a dump on the carpet.

"Try and be a bit more aggressive," the old man said. "You don't get anywhere in cards by acting like an old maid."

"Problem?" I said. "If you'll play with a motherfucker whose face looks like an old hooker's snatch, I can't see why you wouldn't play with me."

"Yeah," said the old man, "maybe not quite that aggressive."

"Fuck you, no tail," said the hairy loser. "This snatch-faced son of a bitch will bite your goddamned head off unless you learn to watch your mouth. I may have lost about ten year's worth of memories tonight, but I don't intend to lose my pride as well."

He squared up to me.

The old man sighed and shook his head. "Can't back down now, that would look even worse. Punch him."

I fair crumbled at that suggestion, made all the worse by the fact I couldn't question it, not without everyone thinking I was even more of a lunatic, talking to thin air.

"Punch him," he repeated, "I'll help."

The dog-faced man loomed in close, his breath as thick and fruity as my old mule's farts.

I figured I was in a fight already, nothing I could say was likely to turn the situation around, so I might as well just join in with conviction. I punched him in the stomach and it was like hitting an old mattress. It clearly hurt me more than him, because he didn't move a muscle.

"In the face, god damn it!" said the old man.

My opponent roared and swung his hairy arm back to return my blow. With what probably sounded like a girl's choir tuning up I shouted back and punched him as hard as I could in his eye.

The old man kicked him in the back of his legs and tugged him backwards by the hair on his head.

Everybody sitting at the table looked as surprised as I did to see the thing fall over. A solid kick from the old man kept him there.

"Yeah," I added, thinking I might as well cash in on this unexpected success. "And stay down, you shaggy piece of shit."

"Don't push your luck, damn you," said the old man, "just sit down and mind your tongue next time."

I took the vacated chair before anyone could argue, and proceeded to try and make friends with everyone.

"My name's..." I had to think for a moment, uncertain of my own name and with only eleven dollars to show for it. "Elwyn," I continued. "Shall we play some cards?"

"I don't tend to play with ruffians," said Agrat, giving me a disapproving look. "I like to keep better company than that."

I looked around the table. As well as her, I was playing with a baby sporting a pair of jet black bat's wings; what looked like a cross between my grandmother and an over-cooked steak, white curls bobbing over its creased, brown, featureless face and what I would have taken to be a carved wooden statue of an Injun were it not currently taking a sip of its drink, fat arm creaking like a tree branch in a high wind.

"I can see that, madame," I replied, "and I can only apologise for speaking so coarsely. Tell the truth, I was bitten by a wolf hound as a child and my tolerance of anything doglike is limited. I guess I spoke out of fear, not thinking of the refined ears that would have to suffer such indignities. If I could take the vulgar comments back I most surely would."

"Not bad," the old man admitted, stood at my shoulder. "I had no idea you knew how to be charming."

Agrat offered a thin smile. "Well, I suppose I might turn a blind eye just this once as you've apologised so sweetly. Now, tell me, are your pockets as rich as your words?"

"Have no fear there, my dear lady," I said, fishing my chips out of my pocket. "Eleven fulsome dollars await your attention."

She laughed. "Oh, maybe I do like you after all, you silly boy. If your memories were only worth that much, I can hardly compound the insult by refusing you a place at my side."

"Oh, is that not very good then?" I looked over towards the kiosk. "Maybe she short changed me."

"Or maybe," said the baby with the bat's wings, "you just didn't live a very full life."

"Plenty of time to change that," I said, but the old man put his hand on my shoulder.

"They think you're dead, remember. And unless you want to cause more fuss than you or I can likely handle, it would be better were it to stay that way."

"Time is gone for you, I think," said the beef-thing in the hairpiece, its meaty skin parting to show a toothless black hole of a mouth. "Life here is a very different thing."

"Which is why we must fill it with games and entertainment," said Agrat. She took hold of my hand. "I take it you haven't played here before?"

"You can tell the truth," said the old man.

I shook my head. "My first time here."

"Then you don't know the traditions of the table," she said.

"Here we go..." muttered the baby with the wings. "I just want to play cards, but now we have to plough through the stories again."

"It's the rules," said Agrat, "whenever someone new joins the game."

"And never let it be said Agrat doesn't like sticking to the rules," the baby replied, rolling its big eyes.

"No. It would indeed be better were that *never* said." Agrat stared threateningly at the baby.

"Fine," it sighed.

Agrat returned her attention to me. "Poker is a game of bluff, but honour demands each person playing should give a brief account of themselves to the other players before the game commences."

"Right, so you know who you're dealing with."

"That's the principle. Though, being a game of trickery

and duplicity, there is no rule that dictates you must tell the truth."

"So I have to tell you who I am, but I can make it up?"

"Of course. Either way, it enables us to get a reading on you. Can we guess whether it's true or not? What does it say about you either way? Poker is all about masks, we ask to see yours. Perhaps it would be better were the others to go first? Perhaps you would care to start, Branches of Regret?"

The thing that looked like a carved wooden man nodded and began to speak.

"I am Branches of Regret," he said. His voice was deep and yet with a constant high whine, the sound of a saw cutting into timber. "I was born when the Navajo came to my forest and wept into the soil. My trees have always fed on the truth of the world and so I was grown. I carry the sadness and anger of a people who have lost a place to put their roots."

"Boo hoo," said the baby. "My name is Axionus and I am of the Forty-First Hellfire Legion. Lucifer took his captured Cherubim and bred them with the darkest, most terrible creatures in his domain. I could kick your ass from here to the Almighty, so don't let the cute looks fool you."

"And I am Brisket," said the meat thing, "and I am the ghost of the slaughterhouse and the kitchen. I am the sharpened cleaver and the fork licked clean."

Finally our hostess: "I am Agrat and I was a lover to the very first man. He could not satisfy me so I made my own way in life."

"Lie," said the old man. It took me a moment to decide whether he meant she had been lying or that I should. I plumped for the latter.

"My name's Elwyn Buckfast, and I am the inventor of the self-cleaning prayer book."

"A valuable invention, I'm sure," said Brisket, bursting into a fit of coughing and spitting that I later understood to be laughter.

"Formalities have been observed," said Agrat, "let's play."

"Ante up, bitches," said Axionus, tossing a fifty cent chip into the centre of the table. We all followed suit and Agrat began to deal for five card stud.

I imagine that my story so far has given you little doubt that I had little experience in the world of card games. Thankfully even I could master the rules of the simplest poker variant. Each player was first dealt two cards, one face-up. The weakest visible card takes the first bet. After that more cards are dealt, face-up, one for each round of betting until each player has five. The area of uncertainty lies in that single face-down card.

I received a hidden eight of clubs and a visible four of diamonds. Not the most exciting hand in the world. Yes, there was the possibility of a straight, but the odds were massively against it. It would all hinge, as five card stud always did, on that hidden eight. The rest of the table looked like this:

AGRAT: 9♥

AXIONUS: 6♣

BRANCHES OF REGRET: 6♥

BRISKET: 3♠

It was down to Brisket to open the betting on the first round, which it did at fifty cents.

Axionus, for all his swagger, folded immediately.

Branches of Regret called on the bet, pushing his chip into the pot with a single, solid finger.

"Raise the bet to a dollar," said the old man. Which had most certainly not been my intention, but I did as I was told.

"I'll call," said Agrat, adding her dollar.

Brisket and Branches of Regret also called, and Agrat dealt three more cards.

AGRAT: 9♥ 5♥

BRISKET: 3♠ 5♠

BRANCHES OF REGRET: 6♥ Q♦

ME: 4♦ 8♥ (8♣)

If all else failed I had a pair of eights.

"Brisket is holding a spade in the hole," said the old man, "aiming for a flush. You don't keep betting if all you've got is a pair of threes, not unless you're a fool and I don't think Brisket is."

In a wig like that, I begged to differ, but kept my mouth shut.

"Agrat can't build a straight flush without the wooden man's six, but she's still on track for a straight. Branches must be holding something worth pairing up with the six for him to have called your bet. Branches is not a bluffer. Whatever he's got, that Queen could be trouble."

Agrat led with the betting, choosing to check.

"No straight, then," said the old man, "the card in the hole ain't a heart, or she'd put some money up. She was willing to call last time, so chances are it's another nine. If so, she beats your pair of eights."

Brisket bet another dollar.

Branches called.

"Call," the old man suggested.

Another card each:

AGRAT: 9♥ 5♥ 2♣

BRISKET: 3♠ 5♠ 10♦

BRANCHES OF REGRET: 6♥ Q♦ 10♥

ME: 4♦ 8♥ (8♣) 8♠

"No chance of a straight for Agrat now, best she has is

a pair of nines. Brisket's lost her flush with the diamond. Branches is still the mystery, but it's probably just a pair of sixes. The hand can be yours, bet high."

I bet two dollars.

"You call two dollars high?" the old man moaned.

I surely fucking did. I'm not a man made of money, and this hand had already cost me over a third of my stake.

Agrat called.

"She's bluffing," said the old man, "or throwing money at you, just to see what you're made of."

Brisket thought about it for a moment, reaching up to scratch at its meaty face with a hand whose nails resembled hooves. Then it folded, as did Branches.

"This is a waste of time," said the old man. "Raise it another couple of dollars."

I did so. Agrat leaned forward and smiled at me. "Are you going to be fun?" she asked. "Or are you going to be careful?"

"A bit of both, I'd imagine."

She nodded and folded. Leaving me now holding more than twice my original stake money.

"Who needs a full and interesting life as long as you can find a bit of luck?" she said, looking at my chips. "Now you're almost worth playing with!"

And play we did, with the old man constantly leading my actions from the rear. The wins were fairly even between us: I lost a few, but won a few too, and after half an hour or so I was looking at a stake of around thirty dollars. This pleased me, having never experienced the false flush of brilliance that comes with getting your hands on money that wasn't yours in the first place. I'll admit, that feeling was going to my head a little; I wasn't used to being a winner.

Then the stakes got high and things began to get scary.

It had come down to me and Agrat, holding four cards each.

ME: 3♣ 6♣ 9♣ 10♣ (with a hidden 2♣ giving me a flush)

AGRAT: 5♠ 5♥ 9♦ 9♠

Which could be a full house or just a two pair. The only way to find out was to brazen the thing out.

Agrat obviously felt the same way about my four clubs with the result being that neither of us was willing to stop raising the bet.

Agrat had a great deal more stake money than I did, and soon it was a case of my having to go all in if I wanted to stand my ground, which, obviously, I did.

"We need to get in the dominant position," the old man said, "or we'll never get what we want from her. She has too much capital."

Which translated as: 'If only you'd been worth more than eleven dollars in the first place.' He wanted Agrat to be in debt to us. It wasn't her money we were after, but her skills, and if we held her over a barrel then she'd be forced to offer them. It seemed to me, therefore, that we needed to alter the state of play some.

"I'm wondering," I said, "whether there might be something else we could use as a stake."

She raised a solitary eyebrow at me. "We are confident, aren't we? What do you suggest?"

"You haven't got anything she wants," the old man said, "not enough anyway."

I ignored him. "As you know," I said, "I'm kind of new at all this, so you'll have to help me along a little. But... what we're staking here are memories and experiences."

"Yes, the only valuable currency here. Most of us have no life of our own anymore, so we take what we can get from others."

"Life," I agreed, "yes. So what if I told you I wasn't actually dead?"

The table erupted in noise at that, not least from the old man. "I told you to keep your mouth shut about that!" he said.

"He can't be," said Brisket, "mortals can't get this far into the dominion with air still in their lungs."

"He's a lying little shit," agreed Axionus. "Probably off his head on Buzz!"

Branches of Regret leaned over, his body creaking. "He is not a liar," he said, "I sensed the truth of his words earlier."

"And chose not to say anything?" Agrat asked with a smile.

"They are his cards to play," Branches replied, "and no business of mine."

"Well," Agrat continued, "how terribly interesting."

"We should tell the manager," said Brisket. "Have him thrown out."

Agrat held up her hand. "You'll do no such thing. I believe the young man was about to make me an offer and I would very much like to hear it."

"Well," I said, "it's just this. I'm a young man with a whole life ahead of me. What might my future experiences be worth? I'm still earning, aren't I? All of this is just more stake in the kitty."

"It is," she agreed, "and it must be said that any man who has walked into Hell while still alive may well have an interesting life ahead."

"Exactly."

"Or... on the other hand, and I think this more likely, he could be dead at any moment and therefore valueless."

"You don't want to follow this line of reasoning, Elwyn," the old man said. "You've blown it. The only way out now is to fold and hope you get out with your life intact."

"Unless, of course," Agrat continued, "you would be willing to agree to an infinite extension."

"No," said the old man, grabbing my shoulders.

"An infinite extension?" I asked.

"Well," she continued, "if I were to take away the possibility of death, then you would continue to accrue value wouldn't you?"

"You're talking about making me immortal?"

"On the understanding that, one day, I was able to take the experience I was owed. It goes without saying I would leave it some considerable time. Where would be the sense in cashing you in quickly? Does that appeal?"

Given the current situation, I had to say it did. After all, if I couldn't die, then I had a distinct advantage in whatever horrors the future might hold. It would mean I had a good few years ahead where nothing could touch me. This is the kind of woolly thinking, I now realise, that gets mortals in trouble.

"And what would you be willing to offer in return?" I asked. "If I were to agree to such a massive stake?"

"What would you like?"

At which point I really needed the old man to tell me, but he stayed silent, moving away from me and standing behind her. He just shook his head.

I had no choice but to improvise. "Well, as I understand it, you stand to gain a whole life of experiences; that's gold, ain't it? It would be the most valuable bet in the room."

She nodded. "I guess it would at that."

"So I should really ask for something huge in return."

"I suppose you should."

I thought for a moment. Looked up at the old man, hoping he would open his mouth. "I'd be open to suggestions!" I joked, trying to give him a nudge. The rest of the players just looked away. It seemed this round of betting had gotten too rich for all of them.

"How about this?" I asked. "If I win I get to ask for one wish... just one... but it can be anything I want?"

"That's so human!" she laughed. "Always full of the old myths and stories. I'm not a genie, young man."

"Fine, but that's the stake. A single request of my choosing."

"But you could ask for my life!" she replied. "Or insist that I was forever enslaved to you! That's too high a stake, even given what you're offering."

She reached for her cards, turning the corner of the hidden card up to look at it. "It was intriguing, and I was tempted by the possibilities, but you ask for too much. Wagers must be precise here, young man, they are utterly binding."

"It's an eight of clubs!" the old man shouted, the most enthusiastic I had ever seen him. "She's bluffing!" He looked at me. "You're an impetuous little shit," he said, "but you do have the winning hand."

"Wait," I could feel I was losing her and, having gone so far, I wasn't willing to back down.

"A single incantation!" the old man insisted. "Ask her for a single incantation. To be used on an unnamed third party."

I repeated his words. She stared at me for a moment.

"A single incantation? That's all?"

"Yes."

"I'm even more intrigued now. I have to know what it is! Very well, the bet is agreed, with the rest of the table as witness. Show your hand."

I did so, revealing my flush.

She looked at it for a moment, then turned over not the eight of clubs that the old man had seen but instead the nine of hearts.

"Damn her..." the old man sighed, stepping back, "Elwyn, I'm so sorry... it was an eight, I swear to you it was eight."

"You cheated!" I said, and all of a sudden the whole room fell silent.

"Be careful, boy," said Branches of Regret. "You cannot accuse another of cheating unless you have proof. Do you have proof?"

I stared at Agrat and the old man behind her. Slowly he shook his head.

"No," I admitted.

"Then take it back," said Agrat, "and quickly, or you'll have worse to contend with than settling your current bet."

I didn't see that I had much choice. "Fine," I nodded, "I take it back..."

There was a sense of relief that passed over the whole room and, slowly, people returned to their games.

"I'll forgive you that outburst," said Agrat, all charm again, "as long as you give me your hand now and settle your debt."

I looked to the old man who was clearly despairing.

I gave her my hand and she took it in her own.

"The house rules are binding," she said. "This isn't just some mortal gambling den, this is a place in the very fundament of existence, and nothing you do can alter the debts owed. I take what you offered. Your life is now mine, to cash in whenever I see fit." She kissed my hand. "And I can assure you it will be many, many centuries from now. I am a very patient woman. You have a long, long life ahead of you. I hope it's filled with things that will one day make my toes curl."

INTERLUDE FOUR
BALLAD OF A GUNMAN

HENRY JONES WASN'T immediately aware that his circumstances had changed. He had spent the last twenty-four hours slipping in and out of consciousness so frequently that his grip on reality was fragile at best.

When his mind was clear enough to make the connection, it made him think of a time when he was seventeen, a young man out on the road and getting in trouble. He had fallen in with a crowd of horse bandits. They'd been fascinated by his blindness (and even more so by his skill with a gun despite what would seem obvious limitations) and they had let him travel with them for a short while. He had never been truly included in the gang's business; they were impressed with him, certainly, but they didn't trust him. He had been more a pet than an equal.

At night, they would cheer him on as he shot cactuses in the dark; a performing monkey that would foreshadow his days in the carnival. One night, just for the devilment, one of the gang, a seedy Texan called Bulrode, had spiked him with peyote to see, or so he claimed: "Whether the young buck can shoot ghosts as well as trees."

Jones had been lost to the world for hours as the psychoactive coursed through his system. He had shouted and screamed so loudly at the visions that had plagued him that the gang had bound his mouth, and he had come close to choking by the time dawn came up and he found himself, once more, in a world he recognised. He had shot Bulrode and ridden the man's horse as far away from the gang as he could.

Those hours in the care of Clarke were not so different. He remembered the chill of the snow that had turned to heat and anger as he carried Knee High, the only member of his gang of outlaws he could find in that white, terrifying world, outside the town of Barbarossa. He had needed the man's eyes, his own ability to sense the world around him lost in the falling curtains of snow that hid his surroundings. He had fought to find his wife, Harmonium, the woman that had always stood by him, despite his moods. He had failed. Like that drug-fuelled night with the horse thieves, time had jumped. One moment he had been in the snow, the next he was lying on his back in a hospital tent. He had wrestled with the doctor, desperate to find out if Harmonium had also been rescued. Then, as the doctor pumped more drugs into his system, he had let go of the world once more, sure of only one thing: his wife was lost to him except in the dreams that followed.

And those dreams were strange things indeed.

He was chasing her through a never-ending graveyard, wooden crosses wherever you turned, spinning round and round in rows that stretched beyond the horizon. He knew, in that way you do in dreams, that Harmonium was buried in one of the graves. So he ran through the rows, ear to the ground, listening out for her. He had to find her soon, before the precious air within the walls of her casket was gone.

The residents of that impossible graveyard were talkative souls. Some encouraged him, some laughed at him, some had the voices of people he had known in his life.

"Run, boy!" one had shouted, with the voice of his uncle. "Run and never stop running, because, when you do, I'll find you!"

You already did find me, thought Jones, *on a sweaty night in Tallahassee when I cut your throat with the neck of a smashed whisky bottle.* The last time his uncle had spoken to him, it had been nothing but hot air and bubbles. The grave had fixed that throat up just fine.

"Henry!" Harmonium had called, and her voice had been choked with earth and grit. "Quickly, god damn you, or I'll never see the light!"

He had run and run and run...

Sometimes he had woken, aware of the sounds of people around him, moaning and crying. The drugs were strong, though, and the moments of consciousness were brief, snatches of air grasped by a man being pulled from beneath by a strong tide.

In some of his dreams, he could see, the skin of his face fallen away to reveal two perfect eyes. Even they were not good dreams. He had been blind from birth and didn't know what to do with the eyes now he had them, didn't know what the colours and shapes that surrounded him meant. They were hard and sharp and looking at them was like running through a forest where the branches kept hitting you and drawing blood.

Then he was with Harmonium, the pair of them lying in the long grass outside Serpent's Creek, the smell of sex and the memory of her body, seen in the best way possible, through the tips of his fingers as they moved all over her.

And then he was stood in the middle of a street.

This, as he would later appreciate, was the moment he truly woke up. At the time he thought it was just another dream, shuffling along through this empty, unfamiliar town.

Normally he could sense the physicality of things around him, he could picture them as rough shapes. The way that the sound changed between wide open spaces and narrow streets, the point at which roofs could no longer enclose the brush of his feet in the dust and opened out into the sky. He didn't visualise the buildings as others saw them—he didn't have the context with which to do so—but he knew them for what they were and could navigate between them easily.

The same went for people. He would hear their breathing, the clothes shifting on their backs, even their hearts pounding away in their chests on the frequent occasion that they saw him and realised their deaths might well be close at hand. This town held no such people; not so far, at least.

Walking was difficult. His legs were weak and threatened to give out, his knee joints wobbling with every step. That and the pain in his hands is what first made him wonder whether this actually was a dream. The visions had been disturbing and surreal, but at least he had moved through them as a whole man, not this fragile remnant, this snapped twig left behind after the snow had melted.

Just ahead of him, he began to sense something. It wasn't a physical object; in fact, it was the absence of one. Just inside a building to his right, there was a patch of space that whined, like Cicadas in the trees. It was a patch of space about which he could tell nothing, and therefore it stood out a mile. He made his way towards it.

Stepping up onto the boardwalk made his hips ache so hard he had to reach out to steady himself. The moment his broken fingers touched the rail by his side, the pain in his hip was subsumed and he fell to the ground, holding his hands protectively out in front of him.

"Not a dream," he whispered. "Pain feels different in dreams."

Slowly, he got to his feet and made his way inside the building.

Once in the same room as that impossible space, that hole in his world, its buzzing was all but deafening. He moved cautiously towards it, trying to map it out, define it by the things he could sense around it. No more than the width of two men, it hung there in the air before him. But what was it? He took another step towards it and felt the hair on his body rise. Whatever it was had power. It was dangerous. It might destroy him. He should certainly not step any closer to it. And yet he did just that. He couldn't say what it was that drew him. In dreams you know the way forward, you cannot help but follow it, however much you might wish to turn another way. Your path is predestined, like a train on its tracks. Even though he was sure now that this was no dream, he still felt that sense of destiny; that there was a line he was following, lead where it may, and attempts to deviate from it would be pointless.

He stepped closer still, the proximity to it making him shake on his unsteady legs. In the end he half stepped, half fell into that impossible, buzzing absence and found himself somewhere else entirely.

He was lying on his front, hands pressed beneath him into the cool dirt. This time they didn't hurt. He rolled over onto his back and held his arms up. His hands were fine; he wiggled his fingers in what was cool night air. Cool night air that bore a familiar smell. This was somewhere he knew well, but he hadn't been here for a long time and the memory was slow to surface.

A short distance away, a fire crackled, and there was conversation and the familiar slap of playing cards. He could smell campfire food and animal cages. Canvas crackled in the breeze, and with it came the memory of where he was. He was back in Dr Bliss' Karnival of Delights, lying next to his trailer after a long day of separating rubes from their money. He couldn't, in all honesty, say that he had loved his time here, but by dint of the fact that he had never loved his time *anywhere*, it was as close as he could get to a welcoming place. Especially if...

"I'm afraid she's not here, Henry," said a voice next to him.

A moment earlier he would have sworn to the fact that he was lying quite alone on the grass. Now he could sense the man that had joined him. He could smell the leather of his boots, the sweat caught up in the fabric of his shirt, the whisky on his breath. He thought back to the man who had first told him about Wormwood; the old drunk who had claimed to once rule the midway with his knife-throwing act (arms bound to his sides, fooling the audience into thinking he had none). The man who had, in short, shaped the last couple of weeks of his life.

"Alonzo?" he asked.

"The same," Alonzo replied, reaching forward and patting Henry on the shoulder. There was the slosh of whisky against glass, and Henry sensed a bottle moving towards him. "Care for a drink?"

Jones did. Taking the bottle cautiously at first, thinking of his hands, then remembering that his wounds were gone, at least for now. This had to be a dream, then, didn't it? Either that or a miracle, and Jones was of a mind that miracles didn't happen to godless sons of bitches like himself.

"We'll find Harmonium," said Alonzo, "I promise you that. I know you want to see her—I know there's little else on your mind but that—but I need you to hear me out first. Can you do that?"

Jones let a mouthful of whisky run down his throat. It burned all the way through him and he rode the sensation like a man floating on the waves of a river. "I guess I can," he said finally.

"You remember the night I first told you about this place?" Alonzo said. "We were sat out here just like this, sharing a bottle and some stories."

"And you were talking about an old gunslinger friend of yours, and how you wondered where he'd fished up."

"That's right, and I talked about Wormwood and how, if a man was strong enough to find his way there, he could walk right into Heaven itself."

"You told me that if I ever found it, I should pass on a message from you to God."

"I did."

"Seems to me that you might just have beaten me to it."

"Honestly? I've always been here. I came to you then, Henry, found you in that carnival because I needed you here."

"I don't follow. You telling me it was all a trick?"

"No, not that. At least, not precisely that. I hunted you out. I had heard of you, and I knew that there was a place here for you. I wanted you to find that place, to be the man you could be."

"Alonzo, I gave up a lot to get here. Everything that means a damn to me."

"No, my friend, that's what I mean. Harmonium can be with you again. You needn't have lost anything. This is Heaven, after all. This is the place where everyone turns up sooner or later. I will make sure the two of you are together again. I can do anything, Henry, if I set my mind to it. Like those hands of yours. They don't hurt now, do they?"

"No," Jones admitted, wriggling the fingers again.

"The wounds of the mortal world are flimsy things, easily swept away. Nothing breaks forever, neither a finger nor a heart."

"And what would you want in return?" Jones was no fool, he'd heard enough promises in his life to know that the good ones came with a big price tag.

"Nothing you wouldn't be happy to give," Alonzo replied. "I'm trying to build something here. Trying to make it a better place. And there's a part for you to play in that, a good part, a powerful part. I have a role for you in mind that would suit your talents right down to the ground."

"You want someone killed? That's usually what people want me to do for them."

"No! Nothing as trivial as that. Though I'm not promising there won't be blood. I want you to rule somewhere for me."

Jones sat up. He was usually good at being able to test the seriousness of someone's words. When all you had was a man's voice, you got skilled at judging the sincerity of it. Alonzo didn't seem to be lying. Nor did what he say make any sense. "Rule somewhere?"

"This place is a world of two halves, Henry. There is Heaven and there is Hell. The latter has become a chaos, a place of chancers, power struggles and division. What it needs is a strong hand, someone to take control of it, to beat it back into shape."

"You want me to run Hell?"

Alonzo laughed. "Yes, my friend, that's exactly what I want."

CHAPTER FIVE
DUCK, YOU SUCKER

1.

I RAN OUTSIDE, thinking, I guess, that I could get some fresh air. Of course, the idea of fresh air in a place like that was madness. The atmosphere was heavy and thick, like leaning over a corpse in the desert.

The deck was virtually empty, most people drawn to the pleasures that could be found inside. I walked towards the rear of the boat, where the paddles cut their destructive way through the horror we sailed on. Over the sound of those heavy blades I heard a low moaning and, in the faint red light of the sky, spotted the dancer I'd found myself obsessing on earlier. She was arched back against the rail, legs apart, while a balding head burrowed beneath the frilly coral of her skirts.

"Oh," I said, both embarrassed and, quite stupidly, angry to see the object of a passing affection busy at such work.

The balding man looked up. He was cross-eyed, his salt and pepper beard glistening. "You want to keep walking, pal?" he said, his voice dreamy but with a clear edge of threat to it. "We're taking care of business here."

I was about to back away when I saw glistening fronds emerge from between the girl's legs' gelatinous appendages that looked like something you'd find on a sea creature. They wrapped themselves around his head and pulled him back to where his mouth could get on with its work.

"Don't mind him," the girl said. "He thinks he's dangerous. Most men do. They learn."

I tried not to stare at the tentacles that bound him, tried not to think where they had come from.

"Sorry," I said. "I just needed to step out a little."

She tilted her head, though whether it was to get a clearer look at me or an involuntary sexual twitch I couldn't rightly say.

"You getting yourself in trouble?" she asked. "Smells like it... I can pick up the scent of most men, you smell kind of... funky."

"I've been travelling," I said. Now mortally embarrassed that I was somehow still conducting a conversation with this girl in the circumstances.

"I don't mean that," she said. "There's something different about you. This place is filled with either those who are dead or those who were never mortal in the first place. Somehow you're neither. It's interesting."

"Oh," I replied, "right... that will be... yeah... I had a bit of bad luck at cards."

The bald-headed man tried to yank his face free from its work again. "God damn it!" he slurred. "Will you just fuck off?" The tentacles pulled him back and, after mumbling a few more indistinguishable threats, he fell silent again.

"Sorry," she said, "a girl's got to feed when she can."

"Feed. Right. I'll just..." I pointed back the way I had come.

"I'll see you again, I'm sure," she said, leaning her head back and closing her eyes. "Look after yourself, strange man."

2.

THE OLD MAN found me at the front of the boat, where I was trying to roll a cigarette. The boat kept rocking and I tried not to imagine it was being pushed upwards by the hundreds of panicked hands beneath us.

"Don't go running off like that," he said. "Not here."

"Why? Not as if anything life-threatening is going to happen to me, is it?"

He looked pained at that, but I'll admit I didn't altogether care. I was feeling sore.

I was also feeling confused. I'll be honest with you, I had been unsettled by what Agrat had said, of course I had, but the idea of immortality still didn't seem all that bad. I had spent the last few days being in almost constant fear of my life; the idea that I wouldn't need to do that anymore was a relief.

Of course, right then, I hadn't really had time for the wider ramifications to sink in. In fact, none of it really had. I was a simple boy who was way out of his depth, and just doing his best to keep his head above water.

"I'll do my best to think of a way around your debt," he said, "but to do that I'll need to get over my own current situation. Which means we still need Agrat and what she can offer me."

"Which is? I figure you can start playing a little straighter with me; what's so special about Agrat?"

"She's a powerful figure, but one that doesn't hold allegiance to the Powers that Be."

"I'm guessing that we're talking about..."

"I told you before, don't say His name."

"Right, yeah... So what can she do for you?"

"She can remove my Non Grata status. As it stands, I can barely exist here. Nobody can see me or hear me."

"You say that like it's a bad thing."

"How would you feel if your identity was removed? That's my curse. I have no name and no presence here. I can't interact with anyone except through a mortal like you."

"You pissed Him off, yes?"

"That's one way of putting it. He made it so that I could never come home, because He saw me as a threat. I was exiled to walk the mortal world, invisible to any of my own kind."

"Having spent a little time with your own kind, did you ever think that maybe wasn't such a great loss?"

"I am who I am, and I want to go home. Agrat can help with that. But she'll only do it if she's forced to do so. We need to have something she wants, we need to be able to trade."

"Well, I'm all out of cash," I said, "and probably about to be kicked off the boat once word spreads that I shouldn't be here in the first place."

"They've got no reason to kick you off," he said. "Even if you were still mortal, that would make you unusual, but you wouldn't be breaking the house rules."

"And what are they?"

"Few and far between. Hell is not a place that thrives in a restrictive atmosphere. There's really only one firm rule onboard this boat..."

"Well, look who it is," said a voice, interrupting the old man. The doors to the casino had opened to release both the desperate mixture of rattling chips and chatter and the floating figure of Axionus. "The poor loser."

"Don't trust him," said the old man. "He may not look like much, but he's a poisonous little shit."

Axionus was flanked by two lumbering heavies. They were both smartly dressed in three-piece suits, but their faces ruined the effect. Flat and charming as tombstones, they were dominated by the teeth in their lower jaws, which jutted out, making them look like walruses who had got a job in a bank.

"I was just thinking to myself," said Axionus, "what brings a mortal to the Bristle?"

"I just love a game of cards," I told him, looking to walk off up the gangway and find a bit of privacy again.

"Don't be rude," the baby-faced bastard said, one of his henchman moving to block my way. "I'm just interested in a little chit-chat."

He hovered in front of my face, his gently-beating wings stirring the foul-smelling air and serving it up to my nose.

"I don't meet a lot of mortals," he said, "not these days. Even during the Fastening they don't tend to end up in these parts. They stick to the tourist areas, I guess. Here? The Bristle tends to be more for locals; you see the same old minor deities, demonic orders and corpses. So, how did you find yourself beating such an untrodden path?"

"Like I said, I was after a game or two. Nothing more to it."

"And what a game, eh? Didn't work out quite as you hoped, I know. That Agrat, she's a tricksy little thing, isn't she?" He fluttered in even closer, an almost overpowering scent of mould and decay seeping from him. "I wouldn't be at all surprised if she *had* cheated. A big no-no here, of course, but if anyone has the chutzpah to try it and succeed, it's her. Still, what are you going to do if you have no proof, eh?"

"Live forever, apparently."

He laughed at that. It was like a toddler choking on its food. "Live forever, yes. It must seem that way to a mortal, but she won't leave you hanging for too many centuries, I'm sure. From experience, mortals really don't get the hang of longevity. After the first few hundred years they tend to find a cave to go slowly mad in. I'd say you'll be at your financial peak in say... three hundred years' time? I'm intrigued, though, what was it you wanted from her that was so valuable you were willing to gamble such a fate?"

"None of your business."

"No, no... I suppose not. But I want to know anyway, I am an insatiably curious little thing. Besides, I am not without power, you know. Anything you might have wanted from Agrat is likely within my power to deliver. Tell me what it was, maybe we can cut a deal."

"He's lying," said the old man. "He's nowhere near powerful enough to do what we need, he's just fishing."

"That really is between me and her," I said. "Now if you'll excuse me I think I'll go back inside and get myself a drink, maybe watch some of the show."

I tried to push past him, but the same heavy that had blocked my path earlier now raised a hefty, cloven hand and pressed it against my chest, pushing me back a foot or two.

"There a problem here, boys?"

I looked over my shoulder to see the dancer I had been talking to earlier. She was now, thankfully, without her suckling attendant.

"There wasn't," sneered Axionus, "but now there seems to be a foul smell in the air."

"That's no way to speak to a lady," I said, without really thinking. I mean, this particular lady seemed to store aquatic creatures in her nether regions and was fond of airing them in plain view. Still, a mother's training dies hard and I was always taught to mind my ways around the gentler sex.

"A lady?" Axionus laughed again. It really was a godawful noise, like a lunatic pumping bellows into a bucket of snot. "You really are new to our world, aren't you? This is no lady, this is a succubus, kid. One of the lower forms. Basically she's a rancid little cooze with ideas above her station. She's also going away, now, or I'll have one of my boys throw her over the side."

"I really don't like your manners," I told him, stepping between the girl and Axionus, like one of the more tender types of idiot. "And you'll have to go through me if you want to lay a hand on her."

"Mind yourself, boy," said the old man. "That's all very sweet, but he's right about one thing. That's not some young innocent whose honour you're defending."

"That's not the point," I said, forgetting nobody else could hear him in my anger. "She doesn't deserve to be called a god damned cooze!"

"It's nice that you're looking out for me, sweetheart," the girl said, taking my arm, "though talking to yourself isn't the best way to impress. Besides, this girl can fight her own battles."

"Will you run along?" Axionus said, his wings beating in agitation. "I am trying to have a conversation here and your smelly quim is putting me off my point."

"Right," I said, having had more than enough of my time on the boat so far. I'd lost all claim to my own life in a hand of cards, been threatened by a dog-faced freak, talked to by an animated pecker and now a baby with wings was rubbing up against every ounce of chivalry I had in me. Young Elwyn was not a man easily provoked, but he was just about fit to pop. "That's as much as I'm willing to hear from you." That said, I punched him right in his stupid toddler's face. He bounced back against the side of the boat, his wings flapping against the windows hard enough to crack the glass.

"Shit," said the old man. "What part of 'mind yourself' did you not understand? You may be immortal, but you're not unstoppable."

The two heavies jumped at me and I managed all of two punches before I found myself heaved up into the air, my legs kicking uselessly.

"If you'd like to shoot them now," I said to the old man, "I won't complain none."

"Can't do it," he said. "House rule number one."

"What?"

"No killing unless in direct self defence."

"This is pretty fucking direct!"

"But they're not threatening me, kid, they're threatening you."

"Tear his fucking legs off!" screamed Axionus, his voice even more sloppy now he had a broken nose to contend with. The blood ran thick and black over his puckered little mouth. "See how he likes that for starters."

At least the girl tried to lend a hand, kicking and slapping at one of the heavies as he tried to get a grip on my leg. It wasn't making much of a dent, but God bless her for trying.

"To hell with house rules!" I screamed. "Shoot the bastards! Please!"

The old man sighed, drew his gun and popped a lovely little bullet into each of their heads.

For a moment there was silence and confusion. Axionus and the girl were confused as to where the sound of gunfire had come from; the two heavies were confused as to why they now had an unwelcome piece of lead just above their eyes, and I was confused as to why I was still being held up in the air.

Then the moment broke as they both toppled over, taking me with them. At least I had a relatively soft landing, coming to rest on their dead bodies.

"What...?" Axionus was fluttering around in panic, his little eyes darting from left to right, trying to see who had fired.

"You weren't talking to yourself, were you, strange man?" said the dancer, helping me up.

"No, I wasn't," I said, "though sometimes it sure feels like it."

"You've really screwed this up now, kid," said the old man, shaking his head. "House rules are taken real seriously."

The air was suddenly filled with the creaking of wood and the gangway began to ripple as planks shifted free from their joists.

"What the hell?" I asked, pulling the dancer close, though more to make myself feel better than to protect her, I'll admit.

"The house polices itself," said the old man, darting forward from the safety rail as it popped loose and, along with the gangway either side of us, curved in on us. The wood splintered to form rough fingers, three makeshift hands grabbing at me.

"It wasn't me that did the shooting!" I shouted.

"Yeah, but it can't see me and you were the one asking for it to happen."

"I was defending my life!"

"You were defending your legs, I guess that's not deemed due cause by the Clearsight."

The wooden hands grabbed me by the wrists, hoisting me back up into the air. The third, which had once been the safety rail, formed a fist with which to punch me in the stomach.

"Strange man," said the dancer, "I like you but I can't afford to fight the house over you. Unless you've got any more tricks up your sleeve, I'm afraid you're on your own."

Which was absolutely charming, given how I'd stood up for her earlier. Not that there was much I imagine she could do to stop a boat beating me up. I mean, it's a boat... how do you fight one of those?

Luckily, there was one man onboard willing to try.

"White man!" came a low, resonant voice I recognised. Looking down I saw Branches of Regret charging through the casino doors—without opening them first, I might add. "You should run now, I think."

3.

DISTRACTED BY A more challenging fight, the parts of the boat that had grabbed on to me let go and swung for the rampaging Branches of Regret. I all but fell off the ruptured gangway and into the soup of bodies we floated on; luckily, the old gunslinger didn't hesitate to help me this time.

"Get a grip," he said, grabbing hold of the back of my shirt as I toppled forward towards open air. I flailed my arms around, desperately trying to find something to hold onto that wasn't likely to hit me.

"You are floating in mid-air," said the dancer, "which is very clever."

"If you could see your way to doing a little less admiring and more helping, I'd sure be grateful."

She reached for my hand and, between the two of them, I managed to get back on more solid footing. Not that anywhere was particularly solid, as parts of the boat continued to peel away from where they had been idly passing the time as handrails, gangway, walls or windows, and began to turn their attention towards Branches of Regret.

My wooden saviour was also undergoing a change. His body stretching and growing, extra limbs sprouting from his solid torso and joining the fight.

"We need to get off this thing!" I said. "While there's still a thing to get off."

"There are a couple of lifeboats on the upper deck, strange man," said the dancer. "Follow me."

She ran along the gangway towards the stairs, myself and the old man following.

We had the advantage of a head start. Most of the patrons were beginning to see that their voyage was taking a turn for the worse, but we made it to a lifeboat before the penny had truly dropped.

"What in tarnation's going on down there?" asked a reptilian looking fellow, popping his scaly head out of his cabin as we ran past. "I'm trying to shed in here."

We ignored him, desperate to get to the lifeboat before we had competitors for what was likely to be limited space.

"Get in," said the old man as we reached it; a small rowing boat with room for all of ten people. "I'll winch it over the side."

I didn't argue, dragging the dancer alongside me and toppling onto the floor of the boat as the old man began to operate the winch that would swing it free of the Clearsight.

"One of us needs to operate the pulley," she said. "I was hoping it might be you."

"That's already in hand," I replied as the boat swung out into the open air and rocked violently from side to side.

"Hey!" called a voice from the deck. "What do you think you're doing there!"

I peered over the side to see one of the crew. I'd never seen a fish with a beard before. If I had I'm sure I would never have seen one this angry. It waved a pair of spindly arms at us; bizarre, flappy things that looked to have been sewn on as an afterthought. "Passengers are not allowed to interfere with the lifeboats!" it shouted just as we dropped, the boat falling through the air as the gunslinger let gravity take its course.

We hit the surface of the Bristle's lake with a terrifying slapping sound, great curtains of ichor flying up at either side. I didn't see the old gunslinger slide down the rope to join us because I was face down in the far corner of the boat, quite convinced I'd cracked my head open.

"Get up, kid," he said. "We need to start rowing."

"Fine, fine..." I shifted myself upright and reached for one of the oars. It promptly reformed into a hand and slapped me in the face.

"The lifeboat is part of the Clearsight," said the dancer, "and it seems to still be angry with you."

"Well you row, then!" I shouted, wrestling to keep the oar from hitting me again.

The old man snatched it from my hands. "Just try and keep yourself to yourself, hopefully the boat won't capsize itself if it thinks it's going to kill her." He nodded towards the dancer. "After all, she hasn't broken any house rules."

"Hey!" came another shout from the deck of the Clearsight. I looked up to see another figure come hurling over the side, jumping through the air towards us. He landed in the middle of the boat, a jump of ten feet or so, squatting perfectly a couple of feet from me. "Room for one more?" he asked. It was the dog-faced card player I'd managed to insult earlier. He recognised me just as I did him and bared his teeth in a snarl. "Well, if it ain't the rude little bastard that got the jump on me. I don't know who it was who gave you a helping hand, no-tail, but unless it was this pretty little thing..."

"I have no idea what you're talking about," the dancer said.

The dog-faced man nodded. "Then I guess we have an even fight this time. Let's see how good you are with nobody to help you by sneaking up on me from behind."

Which is when the old man hit him over the head with his oar before putting the blade back over the side and beginning to row.

"Strange man," said the dancer, rowing as well, "you talk to thin air and people get shot or beaten with no sign of you doing anything. Do you, by any chance, have an invisible friend who is currently helping with the rowing?"

"Something like that," I admitted.

"Good," she replied. "He seems very useful."

INTERLUDE FIVE
HILLS RUN RED

1.

BILLY AND ELISABETH made slow time as they descended the mountain. The light was failing fast and, carrying the body of the woman between them, it was an unsteady journey. Thankfully, concerned for their safety, another party from the camp had set out to look for them. Sat down for a moment to catch their breath, Billy and Elisabeth were relieved to see the bobbing light of lanterns making their way up to them.

"You up here?" called a voice neither of them recognised. "Hello?"

"Hello!" Billy shouted back. "We're not too far above you and thankful of help."

Slowly, the two groups met in the middle, Billy and Elisabeth placing the body of the dead woman before them rather self-consciously.

"I'm afraid we were too late to help her," said Billy.

"We saw whoever it was, leaping up the way there like a mountain goat, but I couldn't get a shot at him."

"Jesus wept," said the man that had been leading the party, holding up his lantern so he could see the extent of the woman's wounds. "He sure made a meal of her didn't he?"

"I don't know if it was him," said Billy, "I was thinking a wild animal of some sort might have got hold of her."

"Were you now?" said the man, looking up at him. "It must have made damn quick work of it."

Billy nodded. "I guess. Just, you know, given the state of her..."

"Ayuh, she ain't pretty." The man looked down at her once more, then held out his hand to shake Billy's. "Dan Simon, tracker back when I was young enough to be any good at it."

"Billy Herbert."

"Elisabeth Forset. Thank you for coming to our aid. It's not been easy carrying her between us. Do you think you might have something we could wrap her up in?"

"Aye," said Simon, "I'm sure we can find something."

"It would be better, I think," continued Elisabeth, "were she covered. I wouldn't want her child seeing her like this."

"I'd say not, she's besides herself enough as it is. Telling the whole camp as how the Devil's among us."

"I dare say that's caused a panic?"

"Yes ma'am, it certainly has."

"Great," said Billy, "just what we need. Tempers were frayed enough as it is. She got any other family?"

"Father died on the way here. We've got one of the Clamshell family looking after her."

"Then maybe we should consider burying her here rather than taking the body back to the camp?" Billy suggested. "I don't think people seeing her like this is likely to help."

Simon thought about this for a moment. "You're not wrong, son," he said, "but I can't speak for the rest of the party behind me, if you know what I mean? There's some who'll be talking the minute they're back amongst their friends, the cat's already well and truly escaped from this particular bag."

2.

IN FACT, THE camp was already whipping itself into a frenzy. The heightened nerves and anticipation following the appearance of Wormwood (and, perhaps even more damaging, the feeling of disappointment that had occurred from the majority being barred from entering) had broken the euphoric mood of earlier. Before the town had appeared, the camp had been a place of harmony. People gathered together in one holy cause. Now there was fear, resentment and confusion. The journey to Wormwood had been hard; many groups had lost members of their party en route. That had seemed tolerable when they thought that paradise was close at hand. Nothing truly worth having came without hardship. If anything, the difficulties all had endured to find their place on that plain had sweetened the arrival of Wormwood. It had assured them that it had all been worthwhile, that they were about to receive their reward. Now, a few short hours later, they still had nothing more to show for their losses than a door they could look at but not open.

As is always the way in such situations, the negative mood of the camp took hold of the first genuine piece of horror and fixated on it. They said the Devil had come to the camp and was stealing the women. A terrifying figure it was, with a red face. It could leap through the mountains that encircled them with supernatural agility. How long would it be before it struck again?

When the news reached the ears of Father Martin—head of the Order of Ruth, that most ancient, unconventional and small of monasterial orders—it hit him particularly hard.

"Tell me again, Brother William," he said to the youngest of the order, "what do they say he looks like?"

"I dare say it has been blown out of all proportion," the novice said, only too aware of the effect his words were having on his elder and dearly wishing he'd never uttered them.

"Perhaps so," Father Martin agreed. "Nonetheless, describe him to me."

"They say he was like a man, but with a bright, red face."

"A red face," Father Martin nodded, "yes."

"Is there a problem, Father?"

"Oh, I think there are several, don't you? Where is one to begin? Where can one even start to consider the sins stacked against us?"

And with that, Father Martin wandered away, leaving Brother William very much concerned for the old man.

3.

THE RESCUE PARTY descended, the body—as per Billy's suggestion—having been buried beneath a pile of rocks a good distance from the camp. The crowd that was there to greet them had already begun to invent what had occurred above them and it was an effort to try and get across the facts.

"I don't know what's wrong with them," said Lord Forset, embracing his daughter. "In the space of an hour people have begun losing their minds."

"They're scared, father," she said, "and resentful. They want something to focus their bad feelings on and our 'devil' in the rocks is the perfect candidate."

"Did you see him?"

"Merely a glimpse, no more than a silhouette as he ran for higher ground. The things he did to the woman though... Oh, father, it was brutal."

He hugged her once more. "I'm sorry you had to witness it, my dear. You should have stayed down here with me."

She bit down on what would have been her normal response to such a statement. He was her father and he didn't mean any insult.

"If you had wanted to spare me the grisly sights, you should have left me at home," she said.

"Would you have remained there had I insisted?"

"Of course I wouldn't."

"Then I suppose we must accept the horrific with the miraculous." He nodded towards the town. "There is still no sign of life from Wormwood. Most people were hoping that a second group would have been admitted by now. It's been nearly five hours since the others vanished and people are mindful of the fact that, within a day, the town will have vanished again. The mood of the camp is not good."

"And the mood of my father?"

"Sore also, I must admit. If I had ever imagined we could have come all this way only to observe from afar..."

"There's time yet, don't give up hope."

"Indeed not. I confess, at the moment, I'm a little more concerned as to what our fellow disciples may do should the situation not change. There have already been a number of fights. Those who know people who have been taken within Wormwood are viewed with hostility by some, as if they have somehow cheated."

"Perhaps we would do well to retire to the Land Carriage?"

"I think so. See if you can help me gather everyone together."

4.

FATHER MARTIN LOOKED up at the mountains, now little more than jagged black absences of stars, and wondered on what might be up there.

Ever since leaving Omaha, he had been plagued with visions of a red-faced man. He had seen him on the street outside their hotel and watched him dance in the dust outside the window of his cabin aboard the Land Carriage. He had considered the man an omen, a warning of some terrible event to come. When poor Brother Samuel had been attacked en route, his body engulfed in hot steam, Father Martin had looked upon the man's pink and blistered face and wondered if that had been the future the vision had predicted. Still, the red-faced man had appeared to him and now he supposed he had his answer. If this creature was the Devil, then what was Father Martin to do about it? The Order of Ruth was an unusual brotherhood, where philosophical thought and biblical interpretation was openly encouraged. Not for them the blind following of well-trodden scripture and universally-held opinion. It was that unconventional attitude that had brought them here, to see the miracle of Wormwood for themselves and explore what it might mean for greater ecclesiastical thinking. If pressed for an opinion before he had begun this voyage, he would have suggested the Devil was a metaphor for the darkness in all men. The part of human nature one had to suppress in order to achieve the divine. That opinion could hardly stand if he looked down on them even now. What should a holy man do? Could Father Martin even claim such a distinction any more? He had seen things, been complicit in actions, on their journey here that made him question his right to the term 'holy'.

As always, the only question one could really consider was this: what would God want me to do?

Father Martin began to climb.

CHAPTER SIX
MAD DOG

WE BEGAN TO pull away from the Clearsight. The boat was losing more and more of its shape as we watched, passengers screaming and panicking all over its surface. I could see the distended form of Branches of Regret, now grown to almost half the size of the boat, his stern profile staring down upon the deck as its countless arms pounded and split. The Clearsight parted at the middle deck, opening up like a snarling mouth, hoping to bite down on its attacker, but Branches of Regret grabbed hold of the upper section and pushed, splitting it even further.

Passengers were doing everything they could to escape: those who could were taking to the sky (I tried to spot the bat-like form of Axionus, but in all the panic there was no sign of him), others were toppling overboard and into the crimson sea.

"Why do you think he did it?" I asked the old man. "Branches of Regret, I mean..."

"Are you talking to me or your invisible friend?" the dancer asked.

"Invisible friend," I replied, "this is going to get confusing..."

"Who can tell with plant entities?" said the old man. "They're a strange bunch. More empathetic."

"I have no idea what empathetic means," I admitted.

"It means capable of seeing, and sharing, the emotions of others," the dancer said, "though I'm sure you probably weren't talking to me."

"They feel things very strongly," the old man continued, "and their allegiances are hard to predict."

There was another almighty cracking sound and the Clearsight began to sink. Branches of Regret now towered over it, an awe-inspiring sight as he pushed the remains of the boat under the surface.

"Well, I like it when he's on my side, that's for sure."

"I'm glad you're happy," the old man said, "though I can't see why. You owe all your future experiences to a demonic entity and we're still no further forward than we were when we stepped onboard."

"Yes, there is that," I admitted. "Fine, it's all gone to shit."

"Are you going to be depressing as well as confusing?" the dancer asked. "Because I'm grateful to have got out of there with my beautiful skin attached but, bearing in mind I wouldn't even have been in the situation if it weren't for you, I'm not sure how patient I'm going to be if you're miserable company."

"Sorry," I said. "It's been a rough couple of hours."

"Meridiana," she said.

"I'm sorry?"

"My name, seeing as you haven't asked yet, is Meridiana."

"Oh, right. Elwyn, sorry."

"Your invisible friend have a name?"

"Sore point. Apparently he pissed someone important off so he's not allowed one anymore. Just like he's not allowed to be seen or heard by anyone except mortals."

"I think I've found myself in a mess."

"You have a bit. So... Axionus, that's the baby with the wings, he called you a succubus."

"He did. You know what one of those is?"

The old man sighed but said nothing, just continued to row.

"No," I admitted, "I'm not really up on all this... Hell stuff."

"Well, I kill people by fucking them. That going to be a problem?"

I didn't quite know what to say to that. "I suppose that depends on whether you plan on... well... you know..."

"You never know; I'm not particularly hungry right now, though. I ate before we came."

"That would have been the bald-headed fellow?"

"A onetime dairy farmer from Ohio. He won't keep me satisfied for long though, the dead never do; they don't have enough life-essence to them, unsurprisingly."

"Right, so..."

"I feed on the life-essence of others through sex. It's how I stay alive. Being stuck here means I get hungry a lot."

"So you might try and kill me in a minute?"

"I might. I'll try to avoid it though if that makes you feel any better."

I sighed and looked at the old man. "We're in a mess, aren't we?"

He nodded. "Though you might want to mention you're immortal until Agrat chooses to cash in her debt. She couldn't kill you if she tried."

"Yes!" I turned back to Meridiana. "You can't kill me, I'm immortal."

She smiled. "Really?"

"Really. It's kind of complicated, but I lost the ability to die in a card game. A woman called Agrat bet against me and cheated. One day she's going to turn up and take all my life experiences as payment. She's made it clear she doesn't intend to do that for some considerable time."

"You're not good at cards, then?"

"She cheated."

"They all say that."

"She really did, my... invisible friend saw her cards and they weren't the same as she played when she won."

"So you were cheating first?"

I hadn't really thought about that. "I guess we were."

She nodded. "I sure know how to find good company."

"Says the woman who kills men by screwing them."

"A girl has to eat."

A large wave, the final result of the sunken Clearsight, pushed against the side of the boat and we rose up in the air before coming back down with a jolt. The dog-faced man groaned in his sleep.

"And who's your friend?" Meridiana asked.

"I don't really know. He's not a friend, though. I accidentally insulted him and then we beat him up."

"You do know that if we weren't afloat on the Bristle lake I would be running away now, yes?"

"Sorry. It all made sense at the time, you know how things can be..."

Above us the sky blossomed with light and another figure appeared, dropping through the red clouds into the lake.

"That's really disgusting," I said, leaning over the side of the boat to look at the lake surface.

"Don't!" both Meridiana and the old man shouted, almost as one. It was good advice, but by the time it registered, something had already burst from the lake and grabbed a hold of my hair. My face was showered in thick blood as this thing tugged at me.

"Get it off! Get it off!" I shouted, pushing against the side of the boat and throwing myself on my back.

My attacker came with me, the upper half of a man, his body just a dripping absence from the waist down.

Meridiana swung her oar at the back of its head and I grimaced as my face was splashed with even more sticky liquid.

The old man slipped the blade of his oar between me and my now immobile attacker, then flipped it back over the side.

"The lake gets lonely," said Meridiana. "Misery loves company."

"I think I'm going to be sick."

"Please don't. It's unpleasant enough in here as it is."

Slowly, we made our way to the shore, finally dragging the boat up onto the hair-covered rocks that encircled the lake.

It seemed too unlikely a coincidence that our dog-like passenger just happened to regain his senses once the hard work was done, but nobody saw fit to mention it. After all, it's hard to complain about a man's work-ethic after you've smacked him over the head with an oar.

"Which one of you cowards hit me?" he asked.

"It was Elwyn's invisible friend," said Meridiana, "so mind yourself or he'll probably do it again."

"How about I just apologise for what I said before?" I offered. "Then maybe we can try and start over?"

I held out my hand to shake his.

He looked at me with a distinctly canine sneer. "I don't know that I'm willing to just roll over..." (which was an opportunity to get the fight started again right there, but I was diplomatic enough not to take it). "I seem to remember you made a pretty foul insult about my face."

"I was stupid," I said. "To be honest with you I was trying to look meaner than I really am, you know? I guess I was showing off a little."

"At my expense."

"Well, yes. But I'm apologising now."

"And that makes it all alright, does it?"

"I'll just hit him again with the oar," said the old man, reaching for it.

"No, don't do that," I said, holding up my hand. "Let's solve this like grown men. I insulted him, he has a right to be pissed off."

"Grown men?" he asked.

"That's right."

So he punched me hard in my face and I fell down into the thick, hairy undergrowth with a rather pathetic cry.

"We're settled," he said. "The name's Biter," he held his hand out to Meridiana. "One of the lower animal entities. Grew up on the south side of Mount Scriven. Don't know if you know the area?"

"I've ridden through it," she admitted, shaking his hand with a slight grimace.

"Yeah, rough part of the world, don't blame you. That's why I got out, trying to make a little something better for myself, you know? I couldn't stand the idea of an existence of cheap summonings or badly paid fright work. A lot of the clans like to hire animal entities as enforcers, but all that barking and tearing people's heads off. It's debasing."

"I'm sure it is." She pulled her hand away. "I'm Meridiana, succubus."

"Oh." He backed away a little. "Right... you're not going to..."

"I'm not into bestiality."

He sighed and looked at me, acting for all the world as if we were now best friends. "See what I mean? This is the kind of intolerance people like me have to put up with. Is it any wonder I have a short temper?"

He suddenly stopped talking and his head snapped to the left, nostrils flaring. "Company coming," he said. "Small convoy, heading this way." He pointed a little way up the shore to where I spotted a narrow road cutting its way through the hairy terrain.

"Let's take some cover," said the old man. "At least until we know who we're dealing with."

"Good plan," I said, getting to my feet. "I'd happily avoid any more trouble for a little while."

The two of us moved towards a small patch of rocks, to the side of the road. After a moment I looked over my shoulder at Meridiana and Biter. "You not coming?"

"He really does talk to himself?" Biter said.

"Invisible friend," said Meridiana, making her way after us, hoisting up the frills of her dress. "Told you."

"Can't smell a thing," said Biter as he too began to follow, "and I can normally pick up even the invisible entities. You know, the spirits, soul hounds and such. This nose has had a lifetime of training, it knows its business."

"I guess nobody here can smell you either," I said to the old man as we settled behind the rocks, keeping our eyes on the road. He didn't bother to reply.

After a few moments we heard the sound of hooves pounding against the sharp, black rock of the trail. Shortly after, emerging from behind an outcrop to our right, three coaches appeared. They rocked on the unsteady ground, the horses that pulled them foaming at the mouth as they galloped along the trail. The coaches were small and ornately decorated, glistening paintwork that seemed to move, like living tattoos. Representations of flames, bizarre creatures, spider-webs and plant-life, all flowing over the coaches' surface. A face appeared at the window of the central coach: Agrat.

"How...?" I began to say, but the old man clamped his hand over my mouth. For a moment I saw her looking out over the shoreline, then her head retreated back inside the coach and they passed us by.

Once they were nothing but a faint dot in the distance, the old man removed his hand.

"Sound travels here," he said, "especially to the powerful."

"Powerful indeed," I said, "considering she managed to get herself off the Clearsight and into a coach without our seeing her."

"She has her ways," he said. "We need to get after her, but I don't recognise the coaches."

"I'll ask," I suggested, turning to Meridiana and Biter. "Any idea who that was?"

"What, Agrat?" said Biter. "You were playing cards with her not half an hour ago."

"Not her, the coaches. You know where she might be going?"

"They belong to Greaser," said Meridiana. "He runs one of the new clans further up the coast. Nasty. I mean... everyone's nasty, but he's a real piece of work."

"Great. We need to follow her."

"You and your invisible friend may need to," said Meridiana. "I sure don't."

"I'm in," said Biter. "She cleaned me out at the table. If there's a chance at getting my own back I'm all for it."

"Who said I wanted company?" asked the old man. "I'm not here to make friends, damn it."

"We'll need all the help we can get," I told him. "Who knows how useful they might be?"

"A hooker and a dog, yes. Helpful." He sighed and began to walk towards the road.

"Please come," I said to Meridiana. "Just for a while anyway; it wouldn't be right just to leave you here, would it?"

"Are you mistaking me for a faint-hearted damsel in distress again?" she said. "I've worked the Bristle for years, there's nothing here to scare me."

"Fine, do as you like." I wasn't going to argue over it. Though I'll admit, I'd still taken a shine to her, even though she was considerably more terrifying than I'd realised when I'd first set eyes on her.

Biter and I set off after the old man, and after a few moments Meridiana followed.

"Don't get the wrong idea," she said. "I just happen to be going this way anyway. There's a small camp a little way up the road; from there I'll make my own way."

She walked a little ahead, as if trying to prove her point. Though it may just have been that she was trying to keep her distance from Biter, who had turned out to be a talkative son of a bitch.

"Thought I'd make my fortune on the boat," he said, "get some capital together. It's hard to bluff someone with senses like mine. I can sniff out bullshit. Both literate and figurish. Didn't quit work out the way I hoped. Just never seemed to get the right damn cards."

"She cheated," I told him. "That might have been a part of it."

"God damn it," he snapped. "I should have known she weren't to be trusted. Any no-tail that smiles at me like that has something to gain. I mean, don't get me wrong, I'm not saying I mind when a woman gives me the eye, but I ain't stupid enough to expect it. The girls don't like the hair. Not most of 'em, anyway. Or maybe it's the teeth." He grinned at me, showing off the intimidating row of incisors. "Who wants to slip their tongue between those, huh? They think I might get hungry and bite it off. Not that I ever would. Well, not usually. There was that time in Madame Hooler's, but I'd been drinking something fierce and I wasn't in my right mind."

"What did you want the capital for?" I asked, anything to get off the subject of his eating women's tongues.

"Well, I figure if I want to make someone of myself I need a clan of my own, you know? Maybe set something up round here, like Greaser. The Bristle seems to be where all the new business is happening."

"What sort of business?"

"The usual stuff, intimidation, torture, a bit of real world trading, though that's tailed off these days. The mortals don't seem as quick to invoke a demon these days. Maybe the Fastening will help this time."

"The Fastening?"

"You don't know much, do you?" he laughed. "The Fastening must be how you got here, no? It's the only time we fix onto the mortal world. Gives us a chance to top up, do a little business, maybe remind a few of you temporaries what's on the other side."

"I never thought about it from this side of things," I admitted. "I guess I just thought it was... I don't know... a miracle?"

"A miracle?" he laughed again. "What does the word even mean? Something you can't explain? You're walking through miracles, son. Nah... We need you lot as much as you need us. The worlds this side need belief, experience, that precious transience you lot have. Don't ask me why He made it that way, you ask anyone in the know and they just give you that guff about 'moving in mysterious ways'. You'd think we had all the power, I mean... what are you but little pink butterflies, flapping about doing fuck all for seventy years and change? But no. We remain beholden to you. It's your belief in us that keeps everything solid, your fear that sharpens our teeth. Major miscalculation on His part, if you ask me."

"I suppose you would say that, though, wouldn't you?" I replied. "Living here. This isn't His place, is it?"

"They're all His places, pinkie. He's the boss of everything. You mortals, the Host, every level of demonic entity, we're all His in the end. They say He always has a plan, not sure I believe it though. Anything about life ever strike you as planned? If you ask me it's a case of too much power and not enough idea what to do with it. We'd be better off without Him."

"Stop talking about Him," shouted the old man. "I've told you before, you're asking to be heard."

I nodded towards the old man. "He's just told me we should change the subject, he seems to think we're asking for trouble if we keep mentioning you-know-who."

"You really got an invisible friend, or are you just insane? I don't mind either way, I've spent time with some real crazies. They're fine as long as you know how they tick. I rode with this guy once, sweet as pie, but if you ever mentioned fruit he'd lose his shit and start killing folks left right and centre."

"Fruit?"

"Fruit. Fucking hated the stuff. Sent him off the deep end, every time."

"I'm not mad."

"He used to say that too, then someone would mention a banana and 'Whoa... limbs everywhere.'"

"I'm really not, though."

"So how comes I can't see or smell him?"

I explained the best I could, repeating what I had told Meridiana earlier.

In the end Biter shrugged. "Best way to hide being mad I ever heard, but I'll go along with it as long as you don't try and kill me."

INTERLUDE SIX
AND HIS NAME WAS HOLY GHOST

1.

HOPE LANE HAD wanted little more from her life than change. From the day she had left her home town, a place that kicked her in the ass every day of her life, she had had no greater ambition than to live a life that was not the one she had originally been dealt. In the first instance, that had seen her change one prison for another, falling into the service of Obeisance Hicks, travelling preacher and crook. He had relied on her utterly, reducing her to a slave; not, she felt, because of the colour of her skin—Hicks hadn't much cared about that—rather because he could. If she had been white he would have treated her no better. Her life on the road with Hicks had been difficult, putting up with his drunken rages, his occasional advances and the fact that she could end up hanging at the end of a rope. If the gullible audiences he preached to had recognised her as part of a con to relieve them of their money, she had no doubt they would have strung her up with pleasure. People didn't like to be fooled, most especially not in the name of God.

For all that, she would not have traded her new life for her old one. The reason why was simple: Soldier Joe.

Hicks had picked the war veteran up in a run down hospital outside Tucson. When spared the potent medication Hicks forced down him—a cocktail of veterinary drugs that he had bought cheap while on the road—the man could be terrifying in his delusions. He would scream and shout at invisible demons, believing he was still under cannon fire or fighting to keep a bayonet from piercing his belly. The hospital had been happy to get rid of him.

"There's nothing we can do for him," the jaded doctor had admitted. "He's a casualty of war, he just hasn't laid down and died of it yet."

But there had always been more to him than just that. Whether it was a result of his injuries or something he had always carried with him, Soldier Joe was a stigmatic, blood flowing from wounds in his wrists. To an imaginative man like Hicks, this was an opportunity of the highest order, and he had been selling vials of calf's blood from the back of his cart (once a piece of rough theatre had convinced all onlookers that the blood came from his troubled messiah) ever since. The one thing Hicks hadn't been willing to do, however, was look after the medical needs of his meal ticket. He was not a man who took naturally to the care of others. So it was Hope Lane, a woman who had always relished the protection of others, that had become Soldier Joe's nurse.

No doubt some would have mocked her for the deep attachment she'd developed for her charge. After all, it was not a love that could easily be returned, Soldier Joe was barely aware of her existence and couldn't, therefore, be said to have any feelings for her whatsoever. Hope didn't think about it. She felt what she felt and that was that. And when she should have died in the snows outside Barbarossa, had her broken man not lifted her in his arms and carried her to safety? They both owed each other their lives, and if that wasn't a foundation for love she didn't know what was.

Now, it seemed, he had brought her somewhere else.

She stood on the streets of Wormwood, looking out across its empty buildings. There, not five feet away, stood Soldier Joe, his wounds dry, his eyes clear.

"Where am I?" he asked her, looking around and scratching at the thick stubble that had grown on his cheeks in the time since she had last shaved him. "I was... in the snow, I think? And then..." He looked at her, not with the confusion that so often came hand in hand with the drugs but with a genuine curiosity, one that held a clarity of thought behind it that she'd never seen in him before. "You were there, I think?" he said. "In the snow?"

"I was," she replied, moving up to him and reaching for his hands. He pulled away slightly, leaving her feeling awkward and a little stupid.

"I know you," he said, but there was no conviction to his voice.

"I'm Hope," she said. "I've looked after you for... well, a long time."

"Looked after me?"

"Yes," she didn't quite know how to address that subject. Was this sudden sense of self-awareness permanent? Was he healed somehow by being here? Or was this just a passing moment? Would he be returned to his broken mind and body any moment? "You were hurt," she said, "in the war... and you needed looking after because there were some things you couldn't do for yourself."

"The war," he said, nodding, "yes. I remember the war. The Confederates hit us on the river, trying to push us back into the swamps. We managed to move north, but the artillery fire..." He raised his hand to his head, his fingers going towards the wound he had sustained there; a wound long gone, replaced by long hair. "I was hurt."

"That was a long time ago, you're much better now." Again she reached for him, again he pulled away.

"A long time ago..." He moved across the street, climbing up the boardwalk and positioning himself in front of the window of a general store. He looked at the reflection he found there—a man with long hair and a beard, styled as a messiah for the appreciation of dumb rubes. It was someone he didn't recognise. "Who are you?" he whispered.

"The war's over," said Hope coming up behind him. "It was over a long time ago. But you were hurt really bad, a bullet to the head."

"How long?"

She didn't know if she should answer that, afraid of the effect the answer might have. Still, she couldn't lie to Soldier Joe. "Twenty years. A little more... I'm sorry, you've been sick a long time."

"Twenty years?" He turned to look at her. "I'm only eighteen..." And then he realised the nonsense of that, the fact that he had lost more than half of his life to a mental fugue. "I got old..." he said, looking back at his reflection.

"I'm sorry, it's one hell of a shock, I know. I wish I could..." What? Make it not have happened?

"Where is this?" he asked, looking around. "Where is everyone? How did we...?"

His legs began to give out and Hope grabbed him, a panic flaring up in her. Not yet! Don't let him fall back into the broken man he had been.

"Come here, honey," she said, struggling to carry him over to the edge of the boardwalk where he could sit down. "Just sit a minute."

"Too much," he said, "can't take it in."

O Lord, she thought, *but we've barely even begun. How am I going to tell him about this place?*

"You were taken from the hospital by a man," she said. "Not a good man. And he used you, as part of his business. But he kept you confused. Gave you powders, drugs."

"I thought you said you took care of me. That doesn't sound like good care..."

"I did my best." She pushed away the surge of guilt she felt a that. "I made you as comfortable as I could, but your head..."

"Yes," he replied, "my head." He reached up to touch it again. His fingers found the rough skin at his temple; the point the bullet had entered.

"You were never right," she said. "It damaged you too much. You didn't know who you were, where you were... You didn't really know anything. But I tried to make it better for you when I could. Tried to make you comfortable." She thought about the cage that Hicks had kept him in, locked up like an untrustworthy dog. "Coming here has changed all that. Coming here has brought you back."

He looked around. "And where is here?"

"It's a place called..."

"Wormwood. It's a town called Wormwood, isn't it?"

"Yes."

"I dreamed about it. I remember that. I dreamed about it all the time. And when I dreamed..." His wrists suddenly began to bleed. Jumping up in panic he stared at the impossible wounds. "What is it? What's wrong with me?"

Hope looked around for something with which to deal with the bleeding. "You're fine," she said, pushing open the door to the general store and scanning the shelves for anything she could use. "Just wait there while I get something to..." She spotted a stack of bed sheets, grabbed one, and stepped back out onto the street.

Soldier Joe had vanished.

2.

SOLDIER JOE DIDN'T know what he was running from. Soldier Joe didn't know very much at all. He just knew that he had to shake off the feelings that were piling in on him, one after the other, before they buried him so deeply he'd never see the light of day again.

As he ran, drops of blood fell from his wrists and pattered into the dust behind him, nourishment to the soil of this impossible place.

He was by no means certain if the things he saw were in his head or tangible presences around him. How could he ever say? Did it even matter? He'd lived in dreams for longer than he'd lived in the real world; he was by no means certain whether one could be said to be more important than the other.

"Praise the Lord!" shouted a fat man stood on the boardwalk next to him. "For he is the bringer of all delights!"

The man vanished, reappearing on the roof of a building to his right. "Can I hear a hosanna?" he cried.

The preacher, Soldier Joe, thought. *Obeisance Hicks.*

As he ran, he remembered the feel of Hicks' leather belt. When the preacher had been too drunk to successfully lash with his tongue he had used his belt instead. Soldier Joe felt ashamed to have been so weak as to let him. To have lain there taking blow after blow.

He wished he could have the preacher here in front of him now. He would have merrily repaid him for every single indignity.

But the girl had said he was dead. So the man that kept appearing out of the corner of his eye must be an illusion, just one more amongst many.

The girl.

She would be panicking now, of course. It was obvious that he was important to her. She wanted to mother him, to keep him under her wing.

Where was his real mother now? His father? Everyone he had known before he had gone off to fight? So many people lost their lives in war, he knew, but most of them didn't go on to truly appreciate the fact.

"Yea, though I walk through the valley of death!" shouted Hicks, standing in the dirt just ahead of him, a Bible in one hand and a mug of whisky in the other.

The valley of death.

He stopped running and looked at his wrists. They had stopped bleeding.

"This is the blood of Christ," Hicks told him, taking a sip of his whisky, "given for you."

Soldier Joe reached out to him, meaning to force that tin mug into his mouth. Hicks was no more substantial than his religious promises.

Wormwood, Soldier Joe thought. *What was so important about Wormwood?*

The valley of death.

Yea, though I walk...

He remembered taking tea with a man on a battlefield. A dream. But important. The man had been called... Had been called...

He had told Soldier Joe he would meet God. That was why he was to come to Wormwood. To meet God.

Alonzo, the man's name had been Alonzo.

Where was Alonzo?

3.

HOPE FOUND SOLDIER Joe stood outside the saloon, staring at the doors. For a moment she thought he had lost the mental clarity he had only just regained, but then he turned to her and she saw that he had simply been deep in thought.

"Sorry," he said. "I shouldn't have run. It was just too much. Still is, really. But I'm trying, one step at a time."

She took his hands, trying to clean the blood from his forearms. He pulled away.

"Don't. It's fine, leave it."

She looked so upset at the thought that he smiled. "It's not personal. You don't have to nursemaid me is all."

He held out his hand. Cautiously, she took it.

"I like to help," she said. "Someone needs to look after you."

"No, they don't. Not anymore. I can look after myself."

Hope tried not to let the fear she felt at that show in her face. After all, she should want him to be well. She just didn't know where that might leave her.

"We need to go in there," he said, nodding towards the saloon. "I'm not sure how I know that, but I do, so there's no point in questioning it. I have enough questions without adding to the list."

Hope looked at the saloon. "What's inside?"

"I don't know. But probably a man called Alonzo. Maybe even God."

She stared at him, not sure what to say to that.

"Don't worry," he said, "I'm sure He'll be pleased to meet you."

He led her inside the building.

4.

THEY FOUND THEMSELVES not inside the saloon but in a large room made entirely of glass.

Soldier Joe stumbled slightly as he crossed the threshold, his immediate impression being that he was stepping out into thin air. Everything was so highly polished that it was impossible to discern the lines. The walls and ceiling were clear, looking out onto sky, but below them the floor was filled with a vibrant world whose perspective changed continually. One minute they were looking down on the empty streets of Wormwood; then the view changed to empty fields; then it changed again, showing the streets of a city, though its buildings were so strange to Soldier Joe's eyes he could barely credit it as such. It was a riot of visual information.

At the far end of the room, reclined on a glass chair, was

Alonzo. In front of him a table was laid for tea, a clear glass teapot making the brown liquid appear to float in a bubble before him.

"Come in, come in!" Alonzo said, standing up. "I've been waiting for ages! I do hope the tea hasn't gone cold." He glanced at it. "If it has, it's easily fixed. If only everything in life was as simple as tea. Perhaps that's why I like it?"

"Alonzo?" asked Soldier Joe.

"You remember me! Excellent, that does make things easier; I was hoping you would." He turned to Hope. "And the lovely Miss Lane, of course. We haven't met, but I could hardly bring one of you here without the other, now, could I?"

He walked forward, feet moving across that maddening floor, now showing a raging ocean, waves reaching up to wash the soles of his boots as he passed.

He took her hand, raised it to his lips and kissed it.

"I hope you don't mind meeting here," he said, sweeping his arm out across the room. "It can be somewhat disorientating to begin with, but once you get the hang of it it's quite simply my favourite place in the whole Dominion."

He sat down, cross-legged on the floor and waved them over, his face suddenly like that of a jolly child. "Come and have a go!"

Slowly, Hope and Soldier Joe joined him, lowering themselves rather unsteadily to the floor.

"I call it the observation lounge," said Alonzo, "because from here you can see everything." He looked up and the smile on his face was smug. "Ever."

"Ever?" Hope Lane asked.

"Absolutely. Well... the future is a little unreliable naturally. You have to take things with a pinch of salt.

What you see one day can be completely different the next. That's what happens when you give mortals free will." He rolled his eyes as if discussing the most basic error imaginable. He seemed to realise this was perhaps tactless, and began to back pedal. "Not that you don't deserve it. Life would be terribly dull for all concerned without it, after all. If we all knew what was going to happen, then where would the fun be, eh? I'm just a bit of a planner, I suppose. I like to be organised."

He waved his hand over the floor and the image of the ocean blurred and began to swirl. "Anyway, forget all that, it gets confusing. Let's start with the basics."

The view below them began to grow clearer. A bird's-eye view of a caravan making its way along a dusty track. The road was lined with plane trees. In the distance a mountain range, further still the beginnings of a small town.

"And... closer," said Alonzo, pointing his palms at the floor and then sweeping them apart. As he did so, the image zoomed in and they were directly above the caravan.

"Hicks," said Hope, recognising it. "But he's dead."

"Not at this point, he wasn't," said Alonzo. "This is a few months ago."

He placed his hands together, finger tips extended towards the roof of the caravan. "Let's take a peek inside, shall we?" He parted his hands and the roof of the caravan appeared to part with them, exposing the inside of the vehicle.

Solider Joe looked down on himself, curled up in the small cage that had been his home for so long. Next to him sat Hope Lane, slowly feeding him a thin-looking stew.

"Ahh," said Alonzo, "isn't she lovely? Who could have asked for better? I wonder what she's saying?" He clapped his hands and suddenly the room was filled with noise, the horses' hooves on the trail, the rattle of the wheels, the creak of the axle.

"Eat up, Soldier Joe," Hope heard her past self say. "It's not much, but it's better than nothing. I make what I can with what he gives me." They watched as she fed him another mouthful. The past Soldier Joe groaned and rolled in her arms, the stew escaping from the corner of his mouth.

"Do we have to watch this?" Soldier Joe asked. "It's awful."

Alonzo shrugged. "It's life. If you get caught up on whether things are nice or not, you'll soon go mad in here. I find it's best just to take things as they come. Nothing stays the same forever." He waved his arm over the floor again. "For example..." The view changed to a vast, white plain of snow. A small dot moved below them. Alonzo repeated the trick with his palms and zoomed in. They could now clearly see Soldier Joe carrying Hope Lane. "Roles switch, lives change," said Alonzo.

He swept his arm across the floor again and now it was the camp outside Wormwood, viewed from a great height. Crowds were sweeping one way and then the other. At this distance it looked like corn moving in a field. Then there was the sound of gunfire. Alonzo sighed and clapped his hands, making the room silent once more. "You lot always fight if we let you."

"If you let us?" Soldier Joe looked at him, a fragment of his dream returning to him. He had been sat with this man observing the battle by the banks of the Tennessee River. The battle that had all but done for him. Alonzo had said something similar then. "You said something like that before."

"Probably," Alonzo admitted. "It's a bugbear of mine, I'll admit. I wish you wouldn't kill each other all the time." He shrugged. "I know it's hard to work against human nature, but there you go, we all have our ambitions. Putting an end to that is one of mine."

"An end to fighting?" asked Hope.

"That's my hope. As I mentioned earlier, I'm a bit of a planner, and it seems to me that with a bit of work, a little nudge here and there, we might be able to get things back on track down there."

Soldier Joe got to his feet, trying not to look down. "I don't know about any of that," he said, holding out a hand to help Hope stand. "This is all a bit beyond me."

"Nonsense," said Alonzo, jumping up. "The human mind is wonderfully elastic. It's terribly good at accepting things. He always found that. I think it rather went to His head at times."

"He?" asked Hope.

"Yes," said Alonzo, moving back over to the tea and beginning to pour out three cups. "You know, *Him*." He handed her a cup and then passed another to Soldier Joe.

"He's not terribly involved these days. He felt it better just to let you get on with it." He picked up his own tea and took a sip. "But my, how He still obsesses, though. It's funny. When He made you, we all wondered what the fuss was. You all seemed so fragile, so..."—he tried to think of the word before apologetically settling on—"pointless. Sorry, I appreciate that probably sounds hurtful. Don't mean it to. It just seemed strange. For millennia, there was just the two dominions, the Dominion of Circles and the Dominion of Clouds." He gestured around them, signifying that in which they were currently standing. "Then came you lot. A lazy afternoon experiment that went on to dominate everything. You're all anyone ever thinks about. And yet there you are"—he pointed at the crowd beneath them—"fighting amongst yourselves and making a shoddy old fist of life, all things considered."

Hope looked at Soldier Joe. "I don't understand a word of this," she said. "I think we should go now."

"Of course you understand," said Alonzo. "You just think it's beyond you, so you hide from it. Stop doing yourself a disservice, woman!" He laughed. "Just go with the flow."

"I've spent my entire life 'going with the flow'," she said to him, "as you well know if you've spent most of yours up here spying on me."

"Oh, not just you," he replied. "I spy on everyone. Only He can claim true omnipotence, but I certainly try my best. The more you know, the better you can plan." He smiled over his tea cup. "And I really have got a terribly good plan. Do you want to hear it?"

CHAPTER SEVEN
FIVE MAN ARMY

1.

WE WALKED THE trail for about half an hour before the smoke and noise of a small camp came into view. The whole place reminded me of a down-at-heel circus that had forgotten to put on a show. The area of beach had been—for want of a better word—shaven of its hair to allow space for people to set up shop. I wondered whether someone had to come out every morning with a razor and strop to keep the ground trim. Tents of varying sizes and quality were dotted about, fires burned, people busied themselves. The camp thrived.

The first port of call, at Biter's insistence, was to get something to eat. It seemed like a fine idea to me; I'd been living off the old man's trail stew for days and something more substantial definitely appealed. At least it did until I saw what was on offer.

"Something hot, my friend?" asked the stunted chef who bounced around behind a pair of cooking fires, shuffling skillets and squirting oil. He looked like a man who been carrying heavy weights all his life, his entire body crumpled like a squeeze box. His face was all about the straight lines: squished, flattened eyes, nose and wide, wide mouth.

"We have the freshest meat available in the whole camp," he assured us. He didn't need to; it was hanging next to him from a pair of ropes, crying.

"Maybe a slice off the thigh?" the chef suggested, showing off his large knife. "Or a whole leg, if you're hungry."

"All of it!" the hanging man begged, his moustache sodden with tears and snot. "It's what I deserve!"

He began sobbing again, his fat belly quivering.

"What do you think?" Biter asked. "Want to share a leg?"

"He's alive!"

"Well, yeah... for now. You prefer belly? Or rump?"

"I prefer something that's not fucking human and crying at me!"

"Oh. Well, it's not like he minds. It's what he wants, after all."

"I do, I do!" the man said looking at me. "Cut me, slice me, fry me!"

"Why?"

This confused him a little. "It's punishment," he said eventually.

"For what?"

"For a life of sin!" he howled. "It's what I deserve!"

"Says who?"

"Him, mostly," said Biter. "This place is full of them. You mortals have a real problem with your lifestyles. Always wanting to be punished for things."

"Well, this *is* Hell."

"Yeah, and you know what they say: Hell is other people." He turned to the chef. "I'll just have some thigh, please."

"Oh, thank you!" the hanging man said. "Thank you!"

"No worries pal, hope it really hurts."

"It will... Oh, yes it will!"

The chef began sharpening the knife. "How do you like it cooked?"

"Barely singed," said Biter. "Just crisp up the edges for me."

I wasn't going to watch, so I chased after the old man, who was on the hunt for transport.

"Lost your appetite?" Meridian asked, catching up with me.

"I don't like to hear my steak scream before I bite into it."

"I know what you mean. Adds sauce, to most of the people you find on the Bristle, though; it's a rough area, you should watch yourself."

"What are they going to do, kill me?"

"There's worse things than dying, Elwyn, don't let your new condition go to your head."

"Yeah, well, you won't have to worry about me for much longer, will you?"

I was feeling all testy, I admit. What with the weird surroundings, the smell of cooking meat and the fact that she'd made it quite clear that she didn't intend to hang around.

Everywhere I looked I saw something disturbing. A man was piercing himself with swords in front of an applauding crowd. Each one bit deeply, and you could tell he was losing his stomach for it. Not least because you could see it, dangling in front of his knees.

Another stall was selling animals, packed into cages so tightly their faces were distorted by the bars. "Divining beast, sir?" the merchant asked as I passed. "Blinded at birth and ready to show you the future in their gizzards at the slip of a knife!"

"No thanks," I replied. "I think I can see my future clearly enough."

"Lucky man," he sighed. "It's all a mist to me."

"Roll up! Roll up!" called another, a massive fellow with a head the size of an apple. Fat hands held a megaphone up to a pinched little mouth, projecting his tiny voice across the crowds and noise. "Who can last in the Tank of Death? Big prizes to anyone who can go the distance!"

Next to him was what looked like a giant fishbowl, seemingly empty until you looked closer and saw a single, brightly-coloured fish darting to and fro.

"I'll give it a go," said a spiky creature with deep, purple skin the colour of a bad bruise. "What's the deal?"

"If you can stay under the water for more than thirty seconds, I'll give you the memories of a mortal President—five years of ultimate power, machinations, blood and thunder! Best memories on the market."

"Alright." The creature tugged off the stained pair of bib pants it was wearing and began to climb up the set of steps next to the tank. "Get that clock running!"

He dropped into the water with a splash, holding his nose closed between pinched fingers. For a moment he just hung there, then he stuck his thumb up to show all was well. The small fish swam around him a few times, then darted at him, and the water was a sudden explosion of internal organs. From clear liquid to gut broth in the blink of an eye.

There was a moment of silence. A small splash. Then the water slowly turned clear again, to reveal the tiny fish had grown massive on its meal. A stream of bubbles ran from its mouth and slowly it began to shrink until the whole tank was just as it had been before—clear water with a single, tiny occupant.

The stall owner raised the megaphone to his face again. "Roll up! Roll up!"

"Why would anyone risk it?" I asked Meridiana.

"People get bored," she said. "They'll do anything to fill their time. These are hard times in Hell; the power base keeps shifting and there's never enough to go round. It's always the same at the end of the Fastening cycle. Everyone hopes things will improve after today, but they never really do. Hell is filled with dead, miserable souls and ever-growing clans. The dead just want punishing, the living haven't got a chance to do anything worthwhile with their lives. It's all just a circus, really."

"Hey," said a small violet giraffe to my left. "Wanna buy some Buzz?"

"I have no idea what that is," I admitted.

"Yeah, yeah," it sighed, "just say no..." He wandered off.

"Buzz?" I asked Meridiana.

"A drug. They say if you take it you feel like a mortal; you get their memories and fears, feel their pain."

"Sounds great."

"It's popular. Tried it once myself, ended up crying about a dead puppy I'd never owned."

As if on cue, Biter caught up with us, his hairy chin now glistening with hot fat.

"You missed a treat," he said. "Best meal I've had in days, rich with pepper and tears."

I just shook my head. This was all too much for me. I looked around for the old man. The sooner we could get out of here, the better.

2.

I FOUND HIM at the far edge of the camp, walking up and down next to a small corral of animals. They bore a similarity to horses, though their skin was black and smooth, more like that of a pig, and their mouths showed a pair of fanged teeth.

"Where've you been?" he asked. "I need you to find out how much it is for a couple of these rakh."

"Rakh?"

"Call them horses if it makes it easier."

"How are we supposed to pay for them? I haven't got anything left to trade with?" I looked to Meridiana and Biter. "I don't suppose you two have any money?"

"Nobody uses money here," the old man reminded me. "It's all about experience or promises. Everyone wants something."

"This ain't a zoo," said a husky voice from behind us. I turned to see a thin, reptilian looking creature, like an Iguana walking upright. "If you want to buy, then let's talk."

"I want four of your rakh," I said. "What's the asking price?"

"We don't want four of them," the old man said, "just two. We ditch the strays here and get on our way."

"Four, is it?" the lizard said. "I have just the beasts you're after. Picked them up in the Thunder Wastes only last night. Run faster than a dog with its ass on fire, so they do."

Meridiana took my arm. "Why are you buying four? You still think you can convince me to come with you?"

I shrugged. "I hope so."

"What have you got to trade?" the lizard asked, giving Meridiana an appreciative look that made me want to yank his forked tongue until it reached his knees.

"I'm about spent out," said Biter, "sorry. Unless you have any intimidation work that needs doing?"

The lizard looked at him. "If I need to scare any folks, I get the wife to do it," he said. "You're in the wrong line of business, son. This ain't the Copper Eventual, we can all do our own intimidating around here."

"What do you want, then?" I asked. "I've probably got some memories you can have."

I was bluffing, I'll admit. While I wasn't struggling too much at that point, my time in the casino had left great, gaping holes in my history, whole months now lost to me.

The lizard beckoned me over, put his hands on my shoulders and then, much to my disgust, his tongue struck me on the forehead as if aiming for a fly. The tongue receded and it looked thoughtful. "You trying to get me in trouble, boy?" it asked. "You're spoken for. I try and lift anything from you and I'm liable to have someone knocking at my door in the middle of the night. You can't sell what ain't yours to give."

"Ask him if he needs anyone killing," said the old man. "If there's one thing I can still do here it's fill someone with lead."

I did so. The lizard laughed. "I've got nobody I need to get rid of. Wish I did, nothing sparks up a dull afternoon like a bit of murder." He looked to Meridiana. "I guess there's maybe one thing I might like to get a taste of though, if you really wanted those rakh?"

"She's not for sale," I said immediately.

"She is if she wants to be," said Meridiana. "She's her own girl, after all."

"Well now," the lizard drew closer. "As long as you folks were of a mind to keep it to yourself... I mean, if the wife heard tell I was trading in such a manner she'd have my tail for a fly swat."

"You can't..." I began to say, but Meridiana turned around and held her finger up.

"Keep quiet," she said. "I know what I'm doing."

She turned back to the lizard. "I'd need those four rakh signed over to us first. I don't mean to come across as an untrusting girl, but business is business."

He shrugged, the folds of loose skin around his throat quivering in excitement as he pulled out a receipt book and began to scribble in it. "I don't mind trusting you," he said, tearing out the receipt and handing it to her. "Besides, you try and pull a fast one on me and I'd just tear your face off." He smiled, showing rows of tiny but sharp teeth. "Now what say you and me head on inside the tent there for a while, while your friends deal with the grunt work? I'll even throw in the saddles."

"You're too kind," she said, following him inside.

At the mouth of the tent she turned back. "Get them saddled up and ready to go," she said, "I'll not be long."

With that, she disappeared.

"I don't like it," I said. "It's just not right."

"Well," said Biter, "he seemed like a bit of a prick to me, so I say he's got it coming."

It didn't understand what he meant. "I was talking about Meridiana, having to have sex with that thing just so we could get some horses... or whatever the hell those things are."

He smirked. "You don't like people getting what they want, do you? You got a real thing about people's dining habits." He wandered over to the coral, looking for the saddles.

"What's he talking about?" I asked the old man.

"She's feeding, boy. And she just solved our transport problem. Maybe it ain't such a bad thing having her along after all."

He walked off after Biter.

3.

THE RAKH WERE like horses in a real pissed off mood. They kicked and snorted and fought to avoid the saddle. I ended up with a mean bite on my shoulder just by walking next to one. After a few minutes I was of a mind that the lizard had got the better bargain, even if he might not live long enough to appreciate the fact.

We'd not long saddled them up when Meridiana reappeared. I tried not to notice the spring in her step.

"We should move," she said. "Who knows when someone will discover the..."

There was a terrible roaring noise from inside the tent.

"Ride now, ride now!" Biter shouted, jumping onto his rakh and kicking at its sides.

The old man followed, Meridiana watching as, to her, a riderless rakh went charging off through the camp. "Your invisible friend," she said. "I don't think I'll ever get quite used to that."

"Never mind him, what the hell is making that noise?"

We both climbed on our beasts as the tent tore in half and a huge lizard appeared. The thing was the size of stagecoach, its mouth wide open, the flaps of its skin quivering as it roared at us.

"I guess that must be his wife," said Meridiana, charging after Biter and the old man.

My rakh refused to move. Even as the giant lizard drew closer, the ground shaking as its heavy feet pounded the earth.

"Move, you fucker!" I shouted, bouncing up and down on the damned thing and kicking at its flank.

It slowly began to trot, in entirely the wrong direction.

The lizard swung its tail at us and it was that that finally got my animal moving, disliking as it did the feeling of a barbed tail up its backside.

Having finally found its running legs, the damned thing was all but uncontrollable, as I rode through panicking crowds.

On either side, angry voices rang out as I nearly ran them down.

"Who taught you to ride?" shouted the owner of the Tank of Death through his megaphone as I charged right at him.

I managed to turn the rakh just in time, but the owner toppled against his tank, upending it. A great plume of water fell over the gathered crowd. One man, a surprisingly dapper young fellow in a three-piece and Derby suddenly clapped his hands together. "It's alright!" he shouted, "I caught it! Somebody fetch me a bowl of..." He then promptly vanished in a red mist, leaving a fat, panting fish lying on the ground where he had been standing.

That was the last thing I saw as the rakh finally caught the scent of its fellows and made a dash for the road.

* * *

4.

After twenty minutes or so of hard riding, it seemed the camp was safely behind us, and we managed to slow our rakh down to a speed that was more forgiving on the ass.

"So I guess I'm sticking with you for now," said Meridiana as I came up alongside her.

"I noticed." I tried to smile, but have a feeling I gave her more of a flatulent grimace. I still couldn't quite get my thoughts straight about her. My mother did warn me that women could be complicated. When she'd said as much, though, I doubt she was envisaging a time when her son might fall for a sex demon.

"After all," she continued, "I guess I do own these things, so it would be stupid not to keep an eye on them."

"I'm trying not to think about that," I admitted. Then went on to prove what I liar I was. "I mean... did it have a normal...? That is to say, it being a lizard, how did you...?"

"Don't worry about it, Elwyn," she said. "You don't always check the straw when you're drinking the iced tea."

The further we went along the shores of the Bristle, the more the landscape began to change, growing flatter and more open. To our left was what looked like an open plain, albeit one of a deep orange hue that made my eyes hurt. The plain was filled with long, covered huts, like cattle sheds. Maybe that was where the lizard thing had kept his rakh?

We were approaching the far end of the lake, where the Clearsight would have happily ferried us had I not inadvertently managed to sink it. There was a small harbour, with a couple of jetties and a shack with strange, unhealthy looking fish hanging from the guttering. As we got closer, I realised they were actually body parts, fished from the lake. Some of them were still twitching.

One last, imposing stretch of rock reached up from the harbour, towering above us. At its summit there appeared to be a large house, surrounded by a high wall, each corner of which featured a guard post. It looked like a fort.

"That's Greaser's place," said Biter. "What a view, huh? He's doing well for himself and that's for sure."

We dismounted, tying our rakh up on a rail by the harbour shack.

"We need a plan," said the old man. "It's not as if we can just go riding on there and ask to see Agrat."

I repeated as much to the others.

"Greaser's main business is in imports and Buzz," said Biter. "People say he has an open channel to the mortal world so he can smuggle goods in."

"What sort of goods?" I asked.

"You're not going to like it."

"I don't like any of this very much. There's no need to start sparing my blushes now."

"Well, according to what I hear—and, you know, this is bar talk, I'll admit that—he's smuggling people."

"People?"

"Not a chance," said the old man. "Demons can travel to your world but you can only travel to ours in very rare circumstances."

"I managed."

"Rare circumstance."

"Excuse me?" said Biter. "You talking to the invisible one right now? Only we was having a conversation and it's confusing as hell when you stop listening and start talking to thin air instead."

"Sorry."

"Maybe we need some kind of signal or something, like you stick your thumbs up and we know to shut up for a minute because someone else is chatting."

"He doesn't really chat. He doesn't think Greaser is smuggling people either. Says we can't travel here under normal circumstances."

"Yeah, well, I know that. Unless you're dead and masochistic or it's the time of the Fastening, those are the rules. Still, that's what people are saying. They reckon he's got friends in high places, you know? Certain authorities turning a blind eye."

"This is the Dominion of Circles," said the old man, "these days the 'authorities' amount to a little more than a couple of corrupt sheriffs."

Biter had been talking so I quickly stuck my thumbs up at him. He rolled his eyes. "Where is this chatty son of a bitch?" He began waving his hands around in the direction I'd been looking. "I swear I'll bite his ass if he keeps interrupting me."

The old man reached forward slowly and punched Biter on the nose.

"Son of a bitch!" Biter grabbed his sore face. "You don't hit dog-based entities on the nose! That's as sensitive as we get."

"Threaten me again and I'll punch you somewhere I bet you're even more sensitive," the old man said.

"He... erm... would rather you didn't try and bite him, is all," I said to Biter, stepping between the two of him. "He gets a bit surly about that sort of thing."

"I'll show him surly! I'll surly the bastard to death if he hits me again."

"Sorry, sorry..." I looked to Meridiana.

"Don't involve me," she said. "I'm just enjoying watching the children play rough."

There was a welcome interruption from the direction of the lake as a sudden splash made us all turn around. A splatter of blood doused the edge of the jetty before two hands thrust upwards and took a firm hold of the planks. Slowly, a figure pulled itself up out of the lake, with twitching, snatching limbs hanging off it like dripping fruit. The figure shook itself like a wet dog, flinging the sorry remnants of the souls from it, and walked towards us.

"Ain't that the woody mother fucker who sank our boat?" asked Biter.

Indeed it was. Branches of Regret, now back to his original size and shape, a wooden effigy of an Indian Chief, stood a few feet from us, dripping blood red in a circle around his massive feet.

"It has been a long walk," he said, "but I am glad to have found you again."

INTERLUDE SEVEN
MINUTE TO PRAY, A SECOND TO DIE

1.

ELISABETH FORSET WOKE to the sound of gunfire.

"Oh, for goodness sake," she sighed, tugging herself out of bed and into her clothes.

She didn't make the same mistake as the day before; to hell with layers of petticoats and dresses. If a day began with the firing of rifles, you had to assume the worst, and she had no intention of facing that in anything less practical than trousers, boots and a shirt.

"What's going on?" she shouted as she stepped out of her carriage and into the passageway beyond. A crowd appeared to have built alongside the Land Carriage, and the windows were filled with angry faces and waving hands. Refusing to make eye contact with any of them until she at least had a vague understanding of what had put them in such a foul temper, she made her way along the corridor and banged on the door of her father's carriage. There was no answer, so she let herself in. There was a time and a place for propriety and it wasn't when there was an angry mob outside your door.

Her father was bundled in his bunk, a pair of wax earplugs firmly wedged into his ears. She shook him by his leg and he awoke with a start.

"Dear Lord!" he shouted. "What's wrong?"

"No idea, father," she admitted, "but we appear to have gathered some unfavourable opinion during the night." She looked across to the other bunk, which was empty. "Father Martin must have arisen early."

"If he did he went to bed late too," said her father. "I haven't seen him since last night."

"That's rather worrying."

The whole carriage shook as the crowd outside pressed against it.

"Not as worrying as that," said Lord Forset. "What the deuce is wrong with them?"

The corridor outside was filling with the Order of Ruth, who very much wanted to know the same thing.

There was a creaking sound and the roar of the crowd got louder. Billy, who slept in a bunk in the engine, had made his way across the roof of the train and descended now from one of the vents in the roof.

"We've got trouble," he said.

"Clearly," Elisabeth replied. "Can you offer any more clues than that?"

"They want to speak to Father Martin. I guess they think he's the closest they have to a spokesman for God."

"He's not here," said Elisabeth, pointing to the empty bed.

"I haven't seen him since late yesterday," said Brother William, stepping into the cabin. "I was talking to him about the stories people were spreading about the Devil in the mountains. They seemed to unnerve him."

"What on earth do they all want?" asked Forset, looking beyond the young novice to the crowd outside.

"They're not happy about the fact that they've heard nothing from the town," said Billy. "People sacrificed a lot to get here. The town's only supposed to be here for a day, and so far, only a handful of people have been able to get inside it."

"Well, naturally," said Forset, "I sympathise with that. I slept in my clothes in the hope that I might wake up somewhere more interesting than my blasted cabin. But why does that make them angry at *us*?"

"We're travelling with men of God," said Billy. "I think their rather twisted logic is that if anyone can tell them what's going on, its them."

"I shall talk to them," announced one of the monks, the aged Brother Clement. "In Father Martin's absence I'm the most senior."

"The eldest," said Brother William, looking at the frail figure. "Yes. I'm not sure that's a wise idea right now."

"My dear child," said Brother Clement, pushing his way past the rest of the order and heading towards the door. "I am a man of peace; I am sure that will be respected."

He opened the door to the carriage and held his arms up before the crowd.

"Please!" he shouted. "Please quieten yourselves. I can't hear a thing if you're all shouting at the same time."

"This is a terrible idea," said Elisabeth, she and Billy moving up behind the old monk.

"We want to know what's going on!" someone shouted from the crowd.

"Don't we all," muttered Lord Forset, shuffling up behind his daughter and Billy.

"I have no more idea than you," announced Brother Clement. "Though I am sure that this is all part of Our Beneficent Lord's plan, a test of patience to see who is truly worthy of the gift of a glimpse of Heaven. Given your current behaviour, I'd say most of you were likely to be struck off the list."

"Oh, no," Billy shook his head. "That won't go down well."

It certainly didn't. A loud roar of disgust welling up from the crowd and a couple more shots were fired into the air.

"There's no good you shouting at me," Brother Clement said. "I suggest you all go back to your tents and pray to God to forgive your actions here this morning."

"He has no idea how serious this is," said Brother William. "I'm going to pull him back in."

But it was too late for that, as another rifle shot rang out.

2.

SCOTT CLAREMONT WAS not a bad man. It seemed to him that he had spent a good deal of his life thus far trying to convince people of that. Yes, he had done bad things, Lord knows he had a temper and there had been times when he had let it get the better of him. Like that night in the saloon on the Wisconsin border, when those idiots had made fun of the South. He had been ashamed of his behaviour that night, but the whisky and the insults had set off a fire in his belly that had burned so brightly it couldn't be ignored. Later, when putting as much distance between himself and the incident as he could, whipping his horse into a frenzy almost to match his own, he had said to himself: *Never again, Claremont; you've just got to learn to control yourself.*

And he'd tried, most certainly he had. He'd kept his drinking within reason and done his best to avoid the sort of situations that fired him up. Still, life was a damned irritant at times and he couldn't always claim to have kept his cool. It was a sickness with him, that was the truth of it. He had tried to explain as much to his first wife as he'd sat on the corner of their bed, nursing his freshly grazed knuckles. Other people were given leave when they fell susceptible to long-held medical problems, people gave them support and understanding. But not him. Nobody seemed to understand he could often not control his temper any more than a man could control his emphysema or dandruff. It was part of who he was, always had been. He wished it weren't the case, but wishing got you nowhere in this world.

He had given it considerable thought on his way to Wormwood. The weeks in the saddle had been conducive to internal examination, and he had very much hoped that finding his goal would be the first step on an even more momentous journey: the road to recovery.

He'd heard about Wormwood during a card game. One of the other men in the camp had laughed to hear him admit that, as if it were an act of sacrilege that his journey had begun in a casino. Claremont was by no means sure of that; he figured God was probably a gambling man. That was certainly the impression he got from looking at the world. Anyway, what did it matter where the journey had begun? What mattered was that he had seen it through. He had ridden through all weathers, seen things he had never dreamed of, even when under the spell of the bottle. In Kentucky he had watched as large crabs roamed the grasses near his ad hoc camp, the night alive with their snapping pincers as they worked through the undergrowth in search for food. He had ridden out of there just in time, the damned things nipping at his back and carving two deep wounds in the rump of his horse. Then there had been the vulture men of Arkansas, he had been convinced that their hideous croak was to be the last thing he would ever hear as they dragged him to their nests on Pinnacle Mountain. If it hadn't been for his speed on the draw, he would have been chick food for sure.

Ever since he had arrived at the camp he had heard stories to match his own. He could only imagine how many people had never made it this far.

All of which made the fact that Wormwood wouldn't let them in beyond his ability to stomach. How could it ignore them all after they had come so far, lost so much? Oh, sure... some had been let inside, though the more you asked around the smaller that number seemed to be. It was like everyone knew of someone who knew someone *else* that might have vanished the day before. During the long, uneventful night (when he had succumbed to the delights of the whisky bottle, yes, and could you blame him?) he had even begun to wonder if anyone had really vanished at all. Certainly everyone he had made a point of talking to since his arrival was still here.

And now this? He hadn't been at the front of the gang that had stormed that weird train, but he'd moved through the crowd, listening to what people had to say. Then the old man had the audacity to say it was their fault? That God had punished them for... for what? Their enthusiasm?

Now that had made Claremont see red, oh, yes it had.

But Scott Claremont wasn't a bad man, no, sir. He had meant to fire that rifle into the air. He wouldn't shoot an old man like that. It was the sun in his eyes. One of the crowd jostled his arm. The rifle always did have a delicate trigger.

Scott Claremont was not a bad man.

3.

THE BULLET THAT killed Brother Clement passed through the bridge of his nose and embedded itself in the ceiling of the carriage, to settle down and rest after a job well done.

"Get the door closed!" shouted Billy, convinced that the shot was only the first of many.

Brother William nearly fell as the dead body of Brother Clement hit him, but managed to grab the old man and pull him to one side as Billy and Elisabeth slammed the door shut.

The crowd outside was momentarily silenced, scarcely believing what had just happened. Then they began to roar once more, waves of anger rising up into the air; anger at everyone and everything, it would seem.

Inside the Land Carriage, things were hardly more restrained. The Order of Ruth—their numbers dwindling— were loudly at prayer, their calm, reasoned approach to theology now swept away in panic, reduced instead to a primal, fearful appeal to God.

Lord Forset was loading his own rifle, hoping not to have to use it but determined to be ready should he have to.

Billy shouted for everyone to stay low in case the crowd took to shooting through the windows.

"Is there any way to lock the door?" he asked Forset.

The inventor, suddenly realising what a mistake that was, shook his head slowly.

"Then we need to think of a way of securing it," Billy continued. He looked at Brother William. "Your belt."

William nodded and immediately began to untie his cincture. Billy tied one end around the door handle while William secured the other against the door of the compartment opposite.

"If they really want to get in," said Elisabeth, "the carriage won't hold for long. They can just smash open the windows."

"Yeah, they can," agreed Billy. "We just have to hope they're too scared of getting their own heads blown off to risk it."

Which was when they looked to the dead body of Brother Clement and it all began to sink in.

4.

FATHER MARTIN HAD spent most of the night walking through the mountain trails. Once his eyes had accustomed themselves to the low light, he had found the going easier than he had imagined. He had also found it bizarrely relaxing. When he had begun his climb, he had been searching for the Devil. Now, hours later, he had found something even more precious: peace.

The last few weeks had seen him consistently trapped outside his normal conventions; travelling with the Order, more often a babysitter than a patriarch, and placed in one violent situation after another. It was a pleasure to climb up out of that world and feel the fresh air in his lungs and silence in his ears (for the most part anyway, the camp was in a raucous mood this evening and the occasional raised voice was brought up to him on the back of the wind). He understood the agitations within the camp, but didn't share them. He had spent his whole life comfortable in the company of a God who didn't feel the need to prove Himself. He was quite happy to imagine the whole affair of Wormwood as nothing more than a test, a reminder that the most important thing about faith was faith itself. That was a Wormwood he could understand and relate to more easily than the showboating Heaven's Gate that everybody else seemed to expect. A symbolic manifestation, a reminder that Heaven was always only a step away, always within reach by prayer.

He sat on a flat rock and watched the sun rise over this miracle in the desert. It made him feel closer to God than he had since he had left the Order's home, all that time ago.

"Makes you glad to be alive, don't it?" said a voice from his left.

He turned and found himself face to face with the original point of his search. The red-faced Devil.

In the flesh, lit by that warm sunrise, he didn't seem quite as intimidating as the gossip of the camp had suggested. He was of average height, dressed in a pair of rough bib pants, almost every inch of his skin etched with tattoos. They seemed, on casual inspection, to be illustrations of animals. His face was pink, yes, sunburned and stained with the blood of recent meals. Not a nice image but not, Father Martin reflected, the face of the Antichrist.

The man smiled and revealed his most bizarre and uncomfortable feature: a set of metal teeth. Father Martin could scarcely imagine the pain involved in having such dentures fitted. Nor could he imagine the reason such surgery would be necessary.

"Don't mind the sight of my gnashers," the Devil said. "I already ate."

Father Martin might have hoped that were a joke, but given the reported state of the woman who had been stolen from the camp, he feared the Devil meant it quite literally. Was it possible this thing had actually eaten parts of her?

"Perhaps we shouldn't talk about that," the Devil said. "I wouldn't want to upset a man of God."

Father Martin was surprised at the lack of sarcasm in the man's voice. "You're a religious man?"

"My folks brought me up right," he replied. "Made me the man I am."

Father Martin wondered if that was intended as a criticism. It didn't seem to have been expressed as one.

"I like to think I've got more God in me than they have, anyways," the Devil said, pointing towards the camp below.

Father Martin watched as a gang marched on the Land Carriage, guns in the air.

"They mean to attack my friends," he said, getting to his feet. "I must go to them."

"You ain't going to get there quick enough to do a spit's worth of use. They've been muscling up for a fight all night. I've been down there, in the shadows, listening to their talk. This has been all night coming, and they'll boil over long before you're halfway down the mountain."

Father Martin accepted the truth of this, even though he couldn't abide the notion of standing by and doing nothing.

"Why are you here?" he asked. "Rather than down there with the rest of us?"

"I prefer to keep myself to myself. I was travelling with a bunch of other folks and we got split up. They left me for dead. I try not to bear a grudge, Father, I know that ain't the holy way, but I figured I'd best keep my distance nonetheless."

"They think you're the Devil, you know?"

The man laughed at that. "Ayuh! I heard that." He nodded towards the mob below them. "You know what I think though? I think the Devil's right down there."

CHAPTER EIGHT
GOD FORGIVES, I DON'T

1.

"YOU FOLKS PLANNING on buying anything, or are you just cluttering my marina up?" The owner of the shack we'd been loitering next to shuffled out of his front door in a mood for a fight. Which was brave of him considering he was all of three foot tall. I'd been here long enough to know that appearances could be deceptive (hadn't I recently seen a fish the size of your little finger eat a man in seconds flat?) but he really was frail looking. His head offered hair so sparse it looked like it had been spun by a dying spider. His face had the youthfulness of a rotting fruit. When he walked he gave the impression that he could tumble at any minute, falling flat on his back, never to move again. Hell, if it came to it, I reckoned even I could take him.

"Some of us are trying to run a business here," he said, walking up to me and fixing me with a stare so wet and dazed I half-thought he might keel over and die right at my feet.

"I would like water," said Branches of Regret, stretching out his massive, stained limbs, "to refresh myself."

"Well now," said the little shopkeeper, "I guess that's a start. Throw in some food and general supplies and it might just have been worthwhile my opening the doors for the day. The Clearsight has usually docked by now, plenty of business there, dang-blasted thing seems to have vanished. Never trust a boat, that's my advice to you."

He turned to waddle back towards his store. "Water pump to the side, you can get your tree washed there. Mind you don't ride off without paying, mind; only an idiot makes an enemy of Mr Benjamin Abernathy. You run off owing me money and I'll hunt you down and take what I'm owed from your corpse."

"Charming," I said, looking at Meridiana. "You planning on screwing him for the bill too?"

"As meals go I reckon he'd be on a par with a dried biscuit and half a cup of rainwater."

"I will pay," said Branches of Regret. "I carry the memories of my entire forest, I am wealthy beyond your imagining."

"Now," I said, "I'm really beginning to like you."

Branches of Regret walked around to the side of the store.

"You know that guy?" asked Biter.

"No more than you," I admitted. "I played cards with him. He seems to have taken a shine to me, though. If it weren't for him, I'd be two legs short and floating face down in the lake."

"If it weren't for him we'd never have had to jump in a lifeboat." Meridiana reminded me.

"True enough," I admitted, "but I still like him."

I turned to the old man. "Why do you think he's decided to partner up with us?"

"Hasn't everyone?" he replied, walking off towards the store. "Ask the owner what he knows about Greaser."

We all followed him inside the store, me giving the dangling body parts wide birth as one fat hand made a grab for my hat.

Inside it was so gloomy it took a moment or two for my eyes to settle. Once they had, I kind of wished they hadn't. It was so full of stock you barely knew where to stand, shelf after shelf of everything from tinned food to cured meats, clothing to weaponry. A large box filled with hair caught my eye.

"Best damn wigs you can buy," said Abernathy. "Made 'em myself."

I lifted one out of the box. It was a strange, mismatched looking thing like a racoon that had been hit by lightning. I tried to shake it into shape and was rewarded with a face full of dust.

"Are they popular?" I asked, dropping it back in the box and trying to brush the dust from my face.

"Never sold a damn one," he moaned. "You just don't get the quality custom in these parts."

"Or enough bald ones?" Meridiana suggested.

"You do a lot of business with Greaser?" I asked, "I see his place is just up the way."

"That piece of shit?" For the first time his confidence wavered. "I say he's a piece of shit... I mean that in the nicest way, of course; you folks work for him?"

"Never met him, don't know him," I admitted.

Abernathy got his confidence back. "In that case he is a piece of shit and I stand by it. His men come riding through here, kicking up a fuss and mussing up my displays. One of those sons of bitches keeps tipping up my postcard rack, takes me a good hour on the step ladders to set them all right again."

I looked at the rack, noting everything from genital close-ups to sketches of war wounds. "Get much call for these?" I wondered.

"Nobody sends cards anymore. People just ain't as communicative as they used to be."

"So you don't sell much to him?" I said, trying to get him back on track with regards Greaser.

"Now I didn't say that. He's a good customer if we're talking in terms of regularity and spend." I couldn't imagine what other terms you could judge a customer on. "He has me take up supplies most every day. Drink, mostly. Smokes. I grow a good approximation of tobacco out back, if I do say so myself. You should get yourself a pouch. It's almost as good as the real thing, once you get over the taste and the bad dreams. Personally I think it all adds to the experience. Want me to fetch you a fistful?"

"That would be great," I said, lying through my teeth, but I felt it was better to try and show willing.

"Good call," he replied. "You won't regret it. Just don't breathe through your nose when you're rolling it and you'll be fine. 'Course, you might like the smell. Old customer of mine swears it reminds him of a dog he used to have. Whether he means before or after it died I couldn't say..."

"Ask him if he's due to deliver anything today," said the old man.

I did so.

"Surely am: three crates of whisky, some jerky and a bale of the tobacco. Fair breaks my back hoisting that up the goddamned mountain and ain't that the truth."

"Maybe we could lend you a hand?" I suggested, catching the old man's eye. He nodded, I'd got the idea.

"And why would you be wanting to do a thing like that?' asked Abernathy. "I thought you said you didn't know the man."

"We don't, but we need to talk to a friend of his about some business."

His screwed-up face screwed up even tighter. He looked like a sphincter after a spicy meal. "What sort of business would that be? You involved in that Buzz trade? I don't rightly hold with all that."

"Oh, no... That's a terrible thing, we wouldn't do anything like that."

He shrugged. "Couldn't give a rat's ass about the drug 'cept it cuts into my whisky and tobacco sales. Those Buzz heads don't touch nothing else."

"No, it's nothing like that. Just a word with a woman that's visiting him."

"Agrat?" he smiled. "I saw her heading past. Now she's a fine woman and that's a fact. She turns my head, so she does, makes me feel like a young man again."

"She is charming."

"A real lady. A woman you'd want to talk to just right. Class. Oh, yes... I'd fair drag my ball sack across a mile of broken glass just to throw pebbles at her shit, so I would."

"That's so romantic," said Meridiana.

He smiled at her. "I can't help it as far as she's concerned. She's just a plum."

"So what do you think?" I asked. "Our help any use to you? We could maybe call it part payment for our goods?"

That did the trick. He grinned. "I knew you didn't have deep pockets. Well, why not? I'm sure we could come to some kind of arrangement."

* * *

2.

WHILE THE OTHERS helped themselves to a few supplies, I went out back to see how Branches of Regret was getting on.

He was stood by the pump, arms outstretched, looking more like a tree than ever. The blood was now all washed off, and all over his body were small green shoots, wriggling as the water ran over them.

"That better?" I asked.

"Much," he nodded, the head moving in that slow, creaky way of his. "It has been too long since I bathed."

"Thanks for helping me out back there," I said. "You got me out of a tight spot."

"And endangered many others doing so," he replied, "because that is the way life works. You choose a side. I have chosen yours."

"That's kind," I scratched my chin. "If you don't mind my asking, why?"

"Memory," he replied, "and sympathy. Are you going to climb the mountain now?"

"I guess we are," I replied, wondering what else to say.

"I will stay here," he replied. "You will find I draw too much attention up there."

"We might need a helping hand," I said. The idea of losing the strong arm of Branches of Regret was... well, kind of regretful.

"You probably will," he agreed, "but I would be little use to you for now anyway. I must recover. Gather my strength."

With that he turned towards the sun, stretched out his arms, closed his eyes and appeared to fall asleep.

* * *

3.

THE TRACK THAT led up to Greaser's place began not a stone's throw from the back door of the general store. It was narrow and uneven, and I had to wonder how any man could do a reasonable amount of business from it. If you're in the import and export trade, doesn't it help if you have a place you can actually take deliveries?

"This is how you do it," said Biter, constantly impressed. "A front door so disinterested in guests, nobody manages to get to it. That's class."

"There must be another way," said Meridiana. "There's no way those coaches got up here."

"This is the tradesman's entrance," said Abernathy, "and we're tradesmen. What do you expect?"

Now it started to make sense.

Abernathy was riding an animal that seemed to be related to the possum. It had a broader back than our rakh, but seemed even less enthusiastic for travel. If I'd been Greaser I might have gone into the horse importing business. Hell seemed very much in need of a beast of burden that didn't resent you at every step.

We'd split the provisions between us, Abernathy's delivery as well as the few things we'd bought of our own. He'd questioned what seemed like a spare rakh, not being able to see its rider, but we had the distinct advantage that he couldn't give a shit about us and therefore didn't care about our answers.

I'd been forced out of politeness to smoke some of Abernathy's foul tobacco, gagging with every breath and trying to keep a smile fixed in place. I imagine a similarly pleasant experience could have been found by setting light to a dead rat and inhaling the result. For the next ten minutes everything looked slightly green. I was in no rush to smoke more.

It took us about half an hour to scale the mountain path. By the time we were at the summit, we had an excellent view of the Bristle in its entirety. If only it had been worth looking at.

There was a large wooden gate ahead of us with a small hatchway in it. Abernathy kicked at the door and stood back, so that he could be seen by the gatekeeper as they opened the hatch.

"Delivery for Mr Greaser," he said. "So open the goddamn door."

"I know you," said the gatekeeper, a skeletal man whose eyelids drooped onto his cheeks like thick, fatty tears. "But I don't know them."

"They're fine," he said. "Just helping me with the delivery because you bastards can never be bothered to collect."

"I'll have to check," he said, slamming the hatchway shut.

"Have to check," sighed Abernathy. "Like there aren't enough gun happy assholes on the other side of the gate to cut us all down in less time than it takes to fart."

"Brilliant," said Biter. "This guy's the business."

After a moment there was the rattle of a heavy chain and a bolt was lifted on the other side. The gate swung slowly open.

I had expected the other side to match the fort exterior; a rough, functional place. The sort of peeling, rundown place hordes of bandits live in. It wasn't that at all.

The gate opened onto a large garden filled with dense bushes, statues throttled by ivy and fat, surreal flowers of a sort I'd never seen before. The colours were all deep reds and purples, making the whole place feel like a floral wound. A wide track led from the gate, through the garden to a huge house at the rear. It was the sort of colonial pile you used to see more of before the Civil War blew so many of them up. The kind of place a rich governor or plantation owner would live in. It had wide balconies and verandahs, huge, glistening windows catching the light from the deep red sun. To the right of the house was another building that matched it for size; I assumed this to be the stables. A group of men of differing species loitered outside it, all of them armed, all of them pointing their guns in our direction.

"Bring it in, then," said the gatekeeper, waving us through.

We rode along the driveway, the men following us with their guns.

"Ignore them," said Abernathy, "they ain't got no manners here."

I looked at the garden to either side, trying to recognise a species an failing. I was no expert, but I was pretty sure none of these blooms had ever grown anywhere but in Hell.

As we drew closer to the house, there came the sound of splashing water. To the left of the trail was a large swimming pool filled with murky, funky-smelling water. This water—or whatever the hell it was; I had decided to no longer speculate on questions I would likely not like the answers to—flowed from the various anatomically precise orifices of statues that surrounded the pool. Human figures, all lovingly-rendered, squatted, thrust or dangled themselves over the edge, keeping the level topped up with their built-in fountains.

A figure was carving its way through the pool, pulling himself along with powerful strokes. When he got to the end, a pair of giant hands slapped down on the tiles at the edge and hoisted him up into the air. This was Greaser.

He was built like a strongman, his entire body a perfect map of muscles and the tendons that linked them. His skin was pale and partially transparent, so you could see the workings beneath. He walked towards us, his bare feet seemingly unconcerned by the thorns and stones they stamped on as he cut through the garden.

"Hello there, Abernathy, you old bastard." He smiled at the little man and his teeth were as perfect as the rest of him, great, shining rectangles that looked like they could snap a finger right off your hand in one happy bite. "You'd better not have short-changed me on the whisky again."

"I never short-changed you before, damn it. I told you, one of your boys here must have taken a swig."

"And who are these friends of yours?" He looked at each of us in turn, Biter about ready to swoon as his attention passed to him.

"It's a pleasure to finally meet you, Mr Greaser, sir," he said, suddenly transformed into a fawning idiot in the presence of someone he found so impressive. "Having heard so much about you."

"Well, ain't that sweet. If I was of a mind to own a pet you'd be first on the list."

That shut Biter up and I felt sorry for him as I watched him bite his tongue.

"And you, darlin'?" he said to Meridiana. "Have you heard all about me too?"

"I sure have," she replied, "but I'm not one to let that prejudice me."

He thought about that for a moment and I wondered if he might just pull her off her rakh and start kicking her until she broke. He certainly looked capable of it. In the end he just decided to keep that fixed smile, turning his attention to me. "And a mortal, I see? Here for the Fastening?"

"And hoping to do a little business," I said.

Here was the thing: the old man and I had discussed our plan at some length while Abernathy sorted out his order. We needed to entice this man somehow and, whether Biter had been right or not in what he had heard, it seemed to us the only way to gain leave to hang around a little while would be to offer some kind of financial incentive. This was a man of business and that was likely the one thing he would respect in someone else, at least as long as he thought there might be a cut in it for him.

"Is that so?" he asked.

Abernathy gave me a dirty look. "Said you were here to see the woman."

"That too," I replied "that too."

"The woman?" asked Greaser.

"I believe the lady Agrat is currently your guest. We have had some past dealings."

"You and the rest of creation, I dare say," he replied, chuckling and patting the neck of my rakh. "That is a woman who gets around."

I wasn't sure what I should say to that, so I simply smiled and kept my peace.

"And what sort of business is it that you might like to discuss?"

"I hear you may be in the market for livestock," I said, "of a rare and valuable breed." .

For the first time he took me seriously. He was by no means convinced of my worth, but I had intrigued him enough to get his attention.

"People talk," he said, "you shouldn't always listen."

"I dare say," I replied, "but as we're here maybe you might have a few minutes for a more private discussion?"

He thought about that for a moment. "I don't tend to do business with people I don't know," he said. "I have something of a temper on me, tell the truth, and I don't like to end up in situations where it's likely to be triggered."

"I'm sure we can discuss things with no fear of that. After all, it's only talk. And later, if you do decide you want to do business, we can worry about credentials then."

He thought for a moment longer, then that big smile returned. "Why not? It's a beautiful day and I wouldn't want it said I don't know how to be hospitable!" He turned to Abernathy. "You and my men get my stuff unpacked and squared away. Then get yourself back down there to your little hole."

"My little hole..." Abernathy muttered, "I'll get you to kiss my little hole one of these days."

Greaser turned back to me. "He's a surly little fucker, ain't he? He's lucky there's no other trading post nearby, otherwise I might be forced to pull that rude tongue out of his head."

He gestured to the stables. "Why don't you let one of my boys stable your beasts and come and join me by the pool for a spell? Maybe you'd even care for a dip?"

"I'm not the strongest swimmer," I said, because there was no way I was setting so much as a toe in that filthy-looking pond, "but I'll happily take the weight off for a while."

"It's a deal." He waved at one of his men, who strolled over. We dismounted and he led the rakh away.

"Oh," said Greaser, looking once more at Biter. "You gonna stable that too? Or do you like to keep it with you?"

"He stays with us," I replied quickly, noting that Biter was having difficulty taking these insults in silence.

"That's sweet," said Greaser. "He maybe do a few tricks? I don't know... catch a ball or something?"

Biter actually coughed at that, trying to swallow back the hollered cures he desperately wanted to offer. He knew better than to put us all in danger, though, and just looked at the ground, his fists clenching and unclenching.

"Sounds like he has a hairball or something," Greaser suggested. "Hope it's not too serious, I'd hate to see it choke to death if you're fond of it."

"That certainly would be a shame," I replied.

I turned to Meridiana. "Maybe it would be best if Biter hang back here?" I suggested. I gave him a look that I hoped he understood as sympathetic. "We don't want to cause anyone upset, do we?"

Biter looked about ready to tear my head off but, in truth, it was him I was thinking of more than Greaser. There would only be so many insults he could take, and I had no doubt that our host would be quick to retaliate, and likely in a manner that ended the argument permanently. Meridiana nodded—she understood, at least—and pulled Biter to one side. The old man followed me as I walked towards the pool, and turned my attention back to Greaser, desperate to move the conversation along. "Shall we take a seat?"

"Surely, let us do just that." He waved towards the house where a maid had appeared. "You folks want something to drink? A mint julep or something?" His smile widened. "I have the sweetest tooth."

"That would be lovely," I said.

"Fetch us three mint juleps, Cassandra, honey," he shouted.

By the side of the pool was a large table. Greaser pointed to one of the chairs and I sat down in it, the old man hovering behind me.

Meridiana, having consoled Biter briefly, sat next to me. I looked over towards the driveway where Biter was clearly muttering to himself and thinking long and hard about what he'd like to do with Greaser.

After a moment our drinks arrived.

"Thank you Cassandra, honey," said Greaser. "You might want to tell our guest we have company, I believe they already know each other."

The maid nodded and retreated to the house.

"You think you can manage this, kid?" asked the old man. I smiled, hoping that was reply enough. After all, it wasn't as if I had much choice, now, was it?

I took a long draught of my drink. It was the nicest thing to have happened to my mouth for weeks.

"So," said Greaser. "Tell me about this livestock of yours."

"Well, as you know, on my side of the fence we did well out of slavery for years," I said. "Then the war came along and attitudes changed. There are some who regret that deeply. Some who have enjoyed the bounty such industry used to pay their families. In the years since that regrettable conflict, fortunes have been spent, certain privileges lost. Then I hear tell that maybe there's someone who might still be willing to do business." I looked at him. "By which I mean you."

"I'd got that," he said, with a laugh. "And what do you think I might be doing with such livestock. If indeed, I am doing anything with it all?"

"Now, that really wouldn't be any of my business, would it?" I replied, taking another sip of my drink. It really was nice.

"I suppose it wouldn't," he agreed. "And what sort of assurance might you be able to offer me that you're on the level?"

"I don't think I'd be stupid enough to come marching in here otherwise," I said, laughing a little too loudly. I put the drink back in my mouth to keep it busy.

"Mint juleps are alcoholic, kid," said the old man. "You might want to go easy on that."

I put the drink down. I'd all but finished it anyway. So that's why I suddenly felt the urge to be really, really loud. When you've made it your business never to touch liquor, you'll find a little goes a long way.

"You'll forgive me—or not, I don't really care—if I say you do seem kind of stupid," said Greaser. "I mean, a wet-behind-the-ears kid, a dog and a dancing girl. It's not exactly the most intimidating posse."

"I wasn't trying to be intimidating; quite the opposite. I'm here to make friends, not enemies."

"Friends, yes... here's another one now." He looked over my shoulder. "Agrat, darlin', I believe you know my young visitor?"

"Brazen it out, kid," said the old man. "It's your only chance."

I stood up, too quickly as it happens, because I became immediately aware that my legs might give way at any moment.

"Madame Agrat," I said, as if greeting an old friend, lifting her hand to my lips. "How lovely to see again so soon! I'm doing everything you suggested and keeping my life interesting."

"So it would appear," she replied, her eyes narrowing slightly as she tried to decide how to respond to me.

"She'll do whatever amuses her most," the old man had said. "That's just the way she is. It's all about the game. You need to convince her that she'll have the most fun by playing along."

"I've just been talking to Mr Greaser here," I said, trying to talk quickly so that she didn't have time to say anything. "Trying to convince him it would be an excellent idea to go into business together. Why don't you come and help? You can tell him what an industrious young fellow I am."

"I suppose I could," she said, sitting down at the table. "But what would be in it for me?"

"A woman after my own heart," said Greaser. "Always looking to the profit."

"Well," I said, "just imagine what fun we could have, if he did decide I was worth investing in! I dare say my life would be one long adventure."

She smiled again. "I dare say."

"That's the trick, kid," said the old man. "She has to decide what's more interesting and valuable to her in the future: you getting a bullet from Greaser in your forehead—for all the good it would do him—or allowing you to continue the pretence."

"So," said Greaser, looking at Agrat, "should I listen to what he has to offer?"

"Oh, certainly. Where would be the fun in doing anything else?"

"She's all about fun," said Greaser, turning his attention back to me. "I think that's the only reason she came knocking on my door. You make a name for yourself and all the women come calling."

"Well, darling," Agrat replied, "that and the fact that I suddenly found myself without transport. When a lady's in need she knows to knock on the most expensive door in reach."

"And that certainly would be mine," he agreed. He turned back to me. "The lady found herself stranded after her boat sank. You hear anything about that?"

"I did indeed," I admitted, before turning to Agrat. "I would, of course, have helped in any way I could."

"I'm sure," she replied.

"So," Greaser drained his drink and slammed the glass on the table, "let's get back to my favourite subject: business. What exactly are you offering me?"

"I'm offering an open channel for livestock between my world and yours, I am in partnership with some of the leading suppliers and we only want to deal with the best over here. I am led to believe that would be you."

"And who is it, exactly, that leads you to believe that?"

"You must be aware that your name has become well known in certain circles."

"I am, indeed, aware; I just want you to start naming those circles. Who have you done business with before? Who can I go to in order to get some sense of your bona fides?"

This was difficult, because, of course, I couldn't name anyone.

"The Greel Enclave," said the old man. "They were always the big movers down here."

"The Greel Enclave speaks highly of you," I said, "and their word, I am led to understand, has weight."

"The Greel Enclave? Really? How interesting."

I looked at Agrat, who was slowly shaking her head. I turned my attention to Meridiana, who had been doing her best to seem invisible throughout the entire conversation.

"Everything's unpacked, boss," said one of Greaser's henchmen, sidling over. "You want me to pay the man?"

"Not really," said Greaser with a smile. "I want you to take him and that dog-faced son of a bitch and tie 'em up in the stables. I'll be wanting to have some fun with them a little later on."

"I don't think there's any need for that," I said, though I could tell I had lost whatever power I might have had.

"I don't rightly give a fuck for your opinion on the matter," said Greaser with a grin. "You're full of shit and I want to know what brought you to my door. The Greel Enclave hasn't been in business for the best part of twenty years. Why, I killed old Changez Greel myself."

"I am a little out of touch," the old man admitted, "sorry. It may be we have to figure another way out of this." He pulled his gun and pointed it at Greaser's head. "Tell him that you have a sharp-shooter ready to empty his brains into that goddamned pool of his unless he lets all of you walk out of here right now."

"You sure that's a good idea?" I asked.

"What's a good idea, boy?" asked Greaser, assuming, sensibly enough, I'd been talking to him. "In my experience any idea I have is, by its very nature, a good one." He leaned forward. "I'm a clever little bastard, you see, that's how I got to be where I am."

"Just do it," the old man said, "afore I have to listen to anymore of his posturing."

"I had hoped not to have to fall back on this, Mr Greaser," I said, "but I'm not so stupid as to come in here unprotected. I have a man with a keen eye and an eager finger training his rifle on you this very minute. If I raise my hand, then he will fire."

Greaser laughed. "Will he now?"

"He will. And let me reiterate: I have no wish to go that route, I just wanted to have a civil conversation, but if that's what it takes for us all to be able to leave this table intact, then that is what I will do."

"Raise your hand," said Greaser, his voice low.

"I'm sorry?"

"You heard me, you little pissant, raise your goddamn hand."

"I can assure you..."

"Assure me fucking nothing..." He turned to his henchman. "Braxis, you and the boys are to do nothing, understand? If this little pecker manages to have me shot, you will let them walk on out of here. You will, in fact, wish them on their merry fucking way. Understood?"

"Sir."

Greaser turned his attention back to me. "So there you go, there's your escape route. All you've got to do is kill me and you walk out of here a happy little band. You can even take the woman with you." He gestured at Agrat.

"Who says she wishes to go?" Agrat asked. "I think you may be assuming a connection between us where there is none."

"I don't care what you think, either. You're all in the same boat, as far as I'm concerned, and you know how that worked out for you last time."

"I don't take kindly to being threatened."

"And I don't take kindly to being lied to." He turned back to me. "So. Raise. Your *fucking*. Hand."

"To hell with it," said the old man, lifting his gun and pulling the trigger. Nothing happened. He pulled again. Silence.

"Raise it!" Greaser screamed and I did so, for all the good I already knew it would do me.

He got to his feet, turning around, holding his head up in the air. "Just so's they can get a clear shot. I wouldn't want them to struggle on that score."

After a moment he sat back down. "I am assuming either you were lying and there weren't no shootist in the first place. Or you were telling the truth and you now know precisely how much use he is to you. Nobody"— he leaned forward, as if I needed this point hammering home, which I most certainly did not—"but *nobody* can hurt me here. This is my home. This is sacrosanct territory. This whole place exists in a state of fucking grace. It would take more power than you've got to break it." He turned to Agrat. "And that goes for you, too, bitch. You may be one of the first family, all-powerful missy, wouldn't stain her knickers Agrat, but my friends are more powerful than you. I am dealing with the real power in the Dominion of Circles, hand in hand with the best, and he looks after his friends."

He leaned back in his chair, relaxed and amused. "So let's get back to our wonderful conversation about livestock, shall we?"

Agrat got to her feet. "It seems clear to me that your disagreement is with this young man, not me. I shall forgive—albeit reluctantly—your threats upon my person, but I certainly don't intend to listen to any more of them."

"Sit down, bitch," he said, his face still at utter peace with itself. "I made it clear enough, I think, you're staying with the rest of them."

"We'll see about that." She closed her eyes and muttered under her breath.

"What's that?" he asked. "Little incantation, is it? Little translocation spell? I heard you could jump limited distances. Pretty impressive. Won't work either. The controlling focus here is my will, that's what the state of grace offers. What I say goes. If I don't want to be shot, I don't get shot. If I don't want you to leave, you don't leave. I can't actually control you, but I can block anything occurring that goes against my wishes. Useful."

"That sort of power isn't for the likes of you," she said.

"She's right," said the old man. "If he's got this sort of protection, he's not bragging about his friends in high places."

"And doesn't it just piss you off?" he said, laughing. He looked at me. "See? You were offering your services as a business partner, I already have the best. Do you have anywhere else to go from there? Didn't think so. On your feet. I'd like to show you some stuff."

We clearly had little in the way of choice, though Agrat was fair fuming at having been proven to be so powerless. She was not a woman you wanted to get on the wrong side of. Unfortunately.

"Thank you so much, young man," she said as she stepped past me. "I can't tell you how much I appreciate the situation you've put me in."

"With any luck," said the old man, "we've put her in exactly the position we need. Tell her if she wants to get out of this she needs to perform a Damnatio Memoriae reversal, when you give her the signal."

I nodded and whispered as much in her ear. She gave me a look that was half surprise, half disgust, but said nothing.

Meridiana took my arm. "You know how I said I wasn't going to come here with you?"

"Yep."

"I'm really wishing I'd not changed my mind."

"I know, sorry."

Greaser led us towards the stables, his henchmen parting to let us past, their hands never far from their guns.

We stepped through a pair of double doors, and the first thing that hit us was the smell. Stables are never the nicest-smelling places, but this was something else. A sharp, painful scent that had my eyes watering as soon as I was inside.

"Takes your breath away, don't it?" said Greaser. "Never smell anything like it. Something to do with the process. Leaking memories, I guess."

Just inside the door I saw both Biter and Abernathy, securely tied and gagged. They seemed unharmed thus far, bar an eye that looked like it was going to blacken up a treat in Biter's case. I wasn't all that worried for them. I had no doubt that whatever Greaser had in mind would be worse for us than them. After all, they were almost beneath his attention.

Greaser pushed open another pair of doors and, finally, we were faced with the cause of the smell.

The room beyond was vast, bigger somehow than it had appeared from the outside. It was lined with row after row of narrow, almost coffin-shaped cages. Hundreds of them. Inside each cage, forced to stand upright, was a naked human—mortals like me, I assumed, given what we knew of Greaser's business. The cages were too small to allow movement, the wires cutting into their skin and forcing it into puffy diamonds. Thin, rubber tubes ran from the heads of each of the prisoners, their tips forced into the skin of their temples, bulging from pink wounds.

"You see?" said Greaser, "I already have all the livestock I need. And this is just my private stock, where I play around and experiment. You may have seen my main farms along the way?"

I remembered the plain we had passed, filled with what I had assumed were cattle sheds. I guess, in Greaser's mind, that's exactly what they were.

"What are you doing to them?" I asked.

"Milking them," he said. "You know about Buzz?"

"I've heard of it."

"It's my main business. Folks just can't get enough of that stuff. Crazy, isn't it? All the power we have here in the Dominion of Circles and yet it's the experience of mortals, that momentary hit, that really fires my customers up. This is where it comes from. I siphon off the memories and experiences of the livestock." He waved at the tubes. "It's then trapped, condensed, distilled—some fucking thing... science is not my skill—and then turned into Buzz. I'm making oceans of the stuff."

I walked up to one of the cages. The woman inside was only being held up by the wire; her legs had grown a deep purple where the blood had settled.

"Hey," said Greaser, running over to me. "Watch this!" He reached up and pinched the rubber tubes with his finger tips. Immediately the woman began to shake, the wire cutting into her even further as she thrashed against it. The side of her head where the tubes went in began to swell. "It gets so that they're producing so much," said Greaser, "something blocks the pipes and they swell up like balloons."

"I get the picture," I said. "You can let go now."

"You get the picture? I don't think you do. I'm going to put you in one of these cages. I'm going to do shit like this to you every day. After a couple of weeks you won't have a fucking clue who you were anymore, at which point I'm going to take you out, mince the fuck out of you and feed you to your buddy next door, if he's still alive. *That's* the fucking picture."

"Ask who's helping him," said the old man.

But I couldn't get a word in, Greaser was on a roll. Now he had put his arm around Meridiana's neck. "And while you're in there, maybe I'll bring this little sweetness along and give you a little show. Would you like that? Just to liven your days up a bit. I could keep those memories of yours topped up a little longer, remembering all the times you'd seen me fuck your girlfriend in her ass."

"She's not my girlfriend," I said, which was about the most pathetic thing possible but I was panicking. Really panicking. I could see that Meridiana was weighing up her response. Like Biter earlier, she was not the sort of person who would take a comment like that in her stride. She likely itched to force the threat back into Greaser's mouth, word by word. At the same time, she knew that she would be dead within moments if she were to try anything. Greaser could probably manage that all on his own, but if he was of a mind not to break a sweat he'd just have one of his henchmen do it instead. We had nothing up our sleeves. Well, possibly nothing; I guessed it would depend on what my old friend could do after Agrat worked her magic. I looked at the old man.

"Ask who's helping him," he repeated. "I want to know."

Greaser, however, was still talking. "Not your girlfriend? Oh, well that's no problem, I'll let you watch anyway." He looked at Agrat. "I may even take a go on you once in a while, though you're going to have to get really dirty if you want me to stay interested, you're a little long in the tooth for my liking."

"How dare you!" she screamed, running at him. She wasn't used to not having the upper hand, and the pragmatism that kept the rest of our mouths shut was lost to her.

Greaser laughed then punched her in the face. *Bam!* That's what he cared for any of us. She fell back into the dirt, holding her hand up to her nose as it started to bleed.

"Ask him, damn you," shouted the old man.

"Who..."—I stumbled on the word, my voice cracking—"who is it that's helping you? Who's your business partner?"

"Say what?" Greaser gave me a quizzical look. "What do you care? I'm telling you all the great things that lie ahead of you and you want to know who I work with?"

"If I'm going to be dead soon, what does it matter?" I said. "It's not like any of us are going to be able to tell anybody."

He stared at me for a moment longer. "Walls have ears," he said in the end, then turned to his henchmen. "One of you give me a gun? I'm beginning to think this little turd ain't taking me seriously enough."

"Now," said the old man as Greaser got a gun.

"Now what?" My legs were shaking, and I stuck out my hand to stop myself falling over. I touched the protruding flesh of the woman in the cage and snatched my hand away.

"The signal. Agrat. Now, damn it!"

"Agrat," I said, but she was in a world of her own, unable to believe what had happened to her. She was staring at the blood on the palm of her hand. "Agrat!" I shouted.

"Right," said Greaser, the gun now in his hand, a heavy looking automatic that he was pointing right at Meridiana. "You say this isn't your girlfriend, yes? So you won't mind if I shoot her in the face? Because I'm happy to do it. Won't dampen my pecker, none. I'll fuck her anyway. Way I look at it, I'm just shooting her a nice new snatch."

I saw Meridiana tense, ready to make a move to defend herself, however hopeless it might be. If she had to go down, she sure as hell wouldn't do it quietly.

"Please Agrat!" I shouted. "Do it now!"

"Do what, kid?" asked Greaser. "Haven't we already covered that you're shooting well below your calibre? It would take more power than that old cunt can muster to make a dent in me."

Agrat began to mutter under her breath.

"So where was I?" Greaser said turning his gun back towards Meridiana. He poked her body with it. "Where do I want the hole?"

"I can tell you where I'd like to put it," shouted Meridiana, as she slammed the heel of her boot down on his bare foot. It had no effect whatsoever. So she aimed a punch at him. He grabbed her wrist and twisted it, forcing her, cursing and spitting empty threats, to her knees.

"I'm beginning to think you people are retarded," Greaser said. "You just don't fucking listen."

He pointed the gun at her face and I ran at him. I knew there was nothing I would be able to do, Meridiana was probably a better fighter than I could ever hope to be, but I couldn't just watch.

Greaser turned to face me, grinning, no doubt full of the joys of what he was about to do to us all. Then Agrat finished speaking and, all of a sudden, the room began to burn.

INTERLUDE EIGHT
IF ONE IS BORN A SWINE

1.

THE GEEK AND his friends walked out into the snow to die.

The real world appeared to have retreated, leaving a small white stage populated by a handful of actors. As well as the Geek, there was Henry Jones; his wife Harmonium; Toby the Snake Boy; the simple-minded veteran called Soldier Joe and his nurse, Hope Lane. All spread out, all waiting for a bullet in the back courtesy of the Barbarossa sheriff, Garrity and Bryson, the barman from the local saloon.

"That's about far enough!" Garritty shouted and the Geek readied himself to run. It would all be about the timing. The visibility out here was so poor that their only hope lay in the time it would take the two men to gun them down. The Geek held his position; to run first was to invite a bullet. He could only hope that one of the others would be the first target, *then* he would run and hope that the snow and the wind would hide him quicker than the sheriff could draw a bead on him.

Then he heard Jones shout: "Harmonium!" His voice barely carried over the wind. "One way or the other I'll find you, honey. Now run!"

This was more luck than the Geek could have expected. Jones had just made himself the primary target. He ran, keeping his body as low as possible without losing his sense of balance, presenting as small a target as he could. Toby ran alongside him, the young idiot.

"Get out of here, damn it!" said the Geek. "We need to split their aim, not make their job easier."

A shot rang out. Then another. Toby gave a yell and fell. The Geek dropped, rolling into the snow. It was so deep he must be all but invisible to their would-be killers. But were they running after him and Toby? Would they be on top of them at any moment?

He turned and looked back in the direction he had run. There was nothing but a pale grey wall of snow and ice.

Then, only appearing when he was almost right on top of him, Bryson was looming over him.

The Geek jumped at the man, making a grab for the barrel of his rifle, pushing it up between them. He didn't have time to think; he responded as nothing more than a cornered animal, leaping onto the startled man and burying his mouth into the soft flesh of his throat. With a grunt, he bit and tore, his freezing cold face suddenly warmed by a jet of arterial blood.

By the time Bryson had registered what was happening enough to make a noise, he no longer had the physical wherewithal to do so.

Holding the man down as he bled out into the snow,

the Geek looked up, a lion keeping a wary eye on the terrain around it before it began to feed.

Garrity must have pursued the others, he decided.

He quickly stripped Bryson of his clothes, the man still choking out his last, and put them on over his own. The more he had to keep himself warm, the longer he might survive. He also took the man's rifle, reloading it from a handful of spare shells in the pocket of the stolen coat. He moved as quickly as he could, only too aware of the fact that he could stumble upon Garrity at any moment.

He tried to listen out for signs of the others, but there was nothing but the wind.

2.

THE GEEK WALKED for an hour or so, by which time even his extra clothing was failing to provide him with warmth. His whole body had grown numb, muscles twitching as he tried to ensure he kept in a straight line. This last had become something of an obsession with him. He was convinced that he was doing nothing more than going round and round in circles. The snow was falling so thickly that he would never stand a chance of seeing his own trail if he came up behind it. The hand of God was sweeping along behind him as he moved, eradicating all sign that he had even been there.

Not that he knew where he was going anyway. He didn't know the area, hadn't the first idea what the lay of the land was like. For all he knew he was walking a straight line that would get him precisely nowhere. Still, that kind of questioning didn't help. His life had become one of absolutes: the snow continued to fall, he continued to walk and he would die or he wouldn't.

He discussed the matter with God, in his simple, unpretentious fashion, and hoped for the best. He knew an acknowledgement of the Lord wouldn't be enough to save him. His parents had filled the air above their sickbeds with Hail Marys and Hosannas, but they'd died in them just the same. Still, it couldn't hurt and it wasn't as if he had anyone else to talk to. So, he walked and he conversed with God. Finally, he even took the gentleman's name in vain as he stumbled through a particularly dense snow drift and found himself face down on hot, dry stone.

He lay there for a moment, pressing his hands to his jaw and cussing, having bitten a small piece off his tongue when he'd fallen. Eventually, he rolled into a sitting position and looked around. He was sat on the top of a mountain plateau, the sun beating down on him as hot as the very fires of Hell. He turned around; there was no sign of the snow he had walked through, and the last signs of it ever having existed fell in small clumps from his clothes and melted on the ground beside him. He stripped off his extra clothes and moved to the edge of the plateau. He was looking down on a small range of mountains, a valley between them and the site of what appeared to be a new town, a growing camp of tents and caravans.

It made no sense at all. But then, that was nothing new.

He needed a rest, but there was no cover from the sun and sitting there in the open was likely to do as much harm as good. He had little choice but to begin the long climb down in the hope he could find somewhere with a bit of shade. He looked at the fading shadows on the rock where the snow had melted and regretted letting it melt away; in this heat he would begin to dehydrate soon and he could have given his body a head start by eating the snow. Too late now; even the shed clothes were all but dry.

He slung the rifle over his shoulder and began to descend. His legs were still far from steady, and he had to go slower than he would have liked, for fear of them giving out.

It took him half an hour to find shade beneath a rock outcrop. He pressed himself beneath it and tried to stop his arms and legs shaking. He closed his eyes, the skin on his face painfully tight as it began to burn.

There was a sudden rattling sound and the Geek realised he wasn't alone. The snake darted for him, but even in his weakened state his reflexes were quick.

"Too slow, Flo," he said, having gripped the snake just beneath its head. It wriggled and thrashed until he took a couple of bites out of it. Hopefully that would give his body a bit of a boost, though, as per his way, he could only swallow a couple of mouthfuls before the animal was dead and, therefore, beyond the state when he could allow himself to eat. Even in his difficult circumstances, he wouldn't break the rule of a lifetime: food had to still be living when it passed your lips.

He fell asleep for a short while, figuring it was best to get his rest now while the sun was at its height.

When he woke, the heat had passed a little as the sun began to fall lower in the sky. He figured it was safe to start moving again.

He crawled out and stretched his legs. They were a little numb with pins and needles, but once he shook them out they felt a lot better than they had before. He was able to get a better speed up now that he felt refreshed, hopping from one rock to another and making his way down the mountain with a precision that would have been the envy of many. Sometimes, the Geek joked about his physicality, the way he could hunt, run and climb. "When you've eaten as many critters as I have," he would say, "some of it's bound to rub off."

In truth he had spent all of his life learning to move like his food; his belly just got fuller that way.

Mid-afternoon, he took a rest and watched Wormwood appear in the open plain before him. It was one of the nicer miracles he'd witnessed. When Alonzo made his announcement, the Geek heard it loud and clear. He suspected it didn't refer to him. He was a witness, not an acolyte.

The attention towards the town offered him the opportunity to deal with his thirst and hunger. The people of the camp were all but absent when he descended.

He had decided that he would keep to his own company on the mountain. He knew from experience that his habits didn't endear him to people.

He found a pair of water canteens hanging from the cross strut of a beige tent. He drank his fill from one and stole the other for later. He had never known such easy pickings. He peered through the flap of a large tent that seemed to be operating as a field hospital—narrowly missing setting his eyes on Henry Jones, Clarke's back blocking his view. It was the only place that still seemed occupied.

He was heading back towards the mountain path when he was punished for his overconfidence.

"Mama!" a young girl cried, suddenly appearing from the other side of a tent. "Monster!"

"Ain't no monster, kid," he said, though his voice was uneven from lack of use and she was far too busy screaming and pointing at him to hear anyway.

"For Christ's sake," he looked around, sure her noise would bring people running any second.

The shovel hit him on the side of his head, bright lights exploding behind his eyes. The rifle fell from his shoulder.

"The Devil!" a woman cried. "Run, baby, it's the Devil!"

That made the Geek see red, damn it. He had spent far too much of his life being called names—and yes, fine, maybe he did ask for it, looking the way he did—but the bitch had nearly caved his skull in. He snatched the spade from her, reversed it and got in a better blow than she'd managed.

He threw the unconscious woman over his shoulder and ran for the mountains, leaving the screaming kid. He could hear she'd begun to draw a crowd and he had no interest in that. Stupid, sloppy work. He dragged her as far as he could, then, aware he was being followed, made an angry meal of her right there in the sun and dust. If they wanted a Devil, he'd damn well give them one.

He avoided his pursuers easily enough, though ended up lying on his back under a rock for several hours shortly after, riotous indigestion twisting his guts to knots.

Then he remembered he'd left the rifle behind. He never had been much good with guns.

As night fell, he listened to the chaos floating up from the camp below him, his stomach still bloated and uncomfortable. He was surprised how much the meat had unsettled him. He wasn't a man with a tender stomach, after all, and you had to learn to scoff when you ate living food. Perhaps it had been the anger he had felt. Or perhaps there had been something wrong with her, something that had poisoned her tissues.

He slept for awhile and, as dawn came, he found he was feeling a little better. The experience had certainly put him off the notion of breakfast, though. Not that he would have considered eating the old man he chanced upon. The meat was too old, the chances of him dying before the Geek even got his teeth wet too high. He simply wasn't of culinary interest. Besides, judging by his clothes, he was a man of God, and his parent's lessons still ran deep. If yesterday's meat had turned his stomach, this would surely tear it wide open.

Instead, they talked for a while. Which was not something the Geek was naturally inclined to do, but the hard night and the morning heat had made him feel dreamy and philosophical.

The old man was concerned over the health of his friends after an angry mob had begun to form. The Geek, having known the power of a mob from time to time, knew that it was too late for the old man to do anything and told him so.

What interested the Geek was how quickly his advice was accepted. For all his initial panic and concern, the old man was clearly desperate to relinquish responsibility for those he considered in his care. Of course, the Geek would happily have told him, nobody is ever really in our care, people will do what they do. Life is a spectator sport, the Geek believed, never more so than when it turns nasty.

"I dreamed of you, I think," the old man said, as the first gun shots rang out below.

The Geek didn't really know what to say to that.

CHAPTER NINE
AN ANGEL WITH A GUN IS A DEVIL

1.

THE ROOM BEGAN to burn.

Greaser had knocked me aside, but almost as an afterthought, his attention now fixed on the point behind me where the old man had stood. He let go of Meridiana's hand too, turning towards the bright flames and the roaring, the point in Hell that was filling with the greatest power that the Dominion of Circles had ever seen.

"What in all the fucks is that?" Greaser wondered.

At the centre of the pillar of fire, the old man stood, his mouth open, the source of the flames that encircled him. His eyes reflected them, but they didn't touch him. Even as they scorched the floor he stood fast, a black shadow at the heart of an orange sun. He was stood with his arms out, palms facing towards his holstered revolvers.

"That's your invisible friend?" asked Meridiana.

"Yeah, though he's not always on fire... I mean, sometimes, a bit..."—I was waffling in panic—"but not like this."

"The Damnatio Memoriae," said Agrat, "now I understand. Of course it would have been him..."

"Oh," I said, "you know him?"

She looked at me as if I were an idiot; not, it must be said, for the first time.

"Of course I know him. Who here doesn't? He's the Fallen, God's Right Hand, The Prince of Hell until his banishing. The Light Bringer."

"Lucifer," added Meridiana.

"Oh," I replied. Just goes to show, you never do know who you're going to bump into on the trail.

He reached for his guns and the moment of stillness broke. His hands seemed to move, gently, almost slowly, but before you could really appreciate the fact, the guns were in his hands and he was firing.

Greaser dived to the right, taking cover in one of the rows between the cages.

"Shoot, damn you all!" he shouted, trying to stir his henchmen from their shock and into action. The old man—Lucifer—needed no such encouragement; three men had fallen in the time it had taken Greaser to speak. His guns barked and the sound was deep, like a dynamite explosion deep underground, a boom that resonated.

"Stay down," said Meridiana, her hand slapping me on the back of my head and forcing my face towards the floor.

I couldn't see what happened next, just heard the wave of gunfire, the screams of the men who took the bullets, the crackle and roar of the flames that encircled the man I had journeyed with all this time.

A wave of heat washed over me as he stood next to us, spent shells raining on our backs.

"Get out of here," he said, and I felt the heat pass as he ran further into the factory, the constant sound of gunfire echoing around the walls.

"I can't believe what you made me do!" Agrat said as we ran for the main doors. "To bring him back... do you realise who I just made an enemy?"

"If He has been paying the remotest attention to your life over the last few centuries," said Meridiana, stooping to pick up the guns dropped by two of Greaser's men, "that can't be anything new."

The main doors swung open and more men entered, alerted by the noise.

"Get down!" I shouted, still in a state of panic.

"To hell with that." Meridiana aimed her purloined revolvers and let rip.

The doorway was filled with flailing dead men and we continued running.

Abernathy and Biter were red with suppressed excitement as we removed their gags and the rope that bound their wrists and feet.

"Did you come up here to start a war?" Abernathy wanted to know. "I trusted you, damn it all!"

"Actually," I admitted, "we came up here to get her"—I looked to Agrat—"to do what she's just done and help my friend."

"What do I care for your friend?" he asked. "I've got a business to run and you're killing all my customers."

"His friend is Lucifer," said Meridiana.

Abernathy's face lit up. "He's back? Why didn't you say? About time, too. This place has gone to the dogs since they kicked him out." He looked at Biter. "No offence."

Biter was too hung up on what Meridiana had said to even notice. "Lucifer?" he asked, nodding towards the factory. "In there?"

"And shooting his way through Greaser's gang."

Biter stared at the closed doors. "What did I say?" he muttered.

"About what?" I asked.

"About your invisible friend! I thought you were just off your head! I didn't know it was him! What did I say? Have I offended him? Is he going to come out here and kill me next?"

"I wouldn't have thought so."

"Maybe I should just shoot myself anyway. Try and get on his good side."

"I'd be happy to help," said Agrat.

"Nobody's shooting anybody but me," said Meridiana, heading towards the door. "Now let's get out in the open."

"Shouldn't we give him a hand?" I asked, looking towards the continued sound of gunfire.

"Elwyn, honey," she said, "he's the most powerful being, bar one, in existence. He don't need your help."

We stepped outside, Meridiana waving for us to keep back against the wall of the building. "Greaser had a whole army up here," she said. "They could be pointing their guns at us right now."

"The house," I said. "We can take cover there."

As we ran, we heard shouts coming from the far side of the building. The noise from the factory had finally raised alarm bells.

Abernathy led the way, pushing open the front door of the house and waving us all inside.

"Doubt he has his hired guns in the home," said Biter.

"A man of class wouldn't do that. Servants, yes—there'll be plenty of those—but he'll keep the others out."

"Then this is definitely the best place to be," agreed Meridiana.

"Upstairs," said Agrat. "From the verandah we can see what's going on." She began to walk ahead, then stopped and turned. "Well? Come on then! Need I remind you that I know my way around? Some of us were here as guests."

One of the maids—to my embarrassment I cannot say if it was the same one who brought me my drink; I wasn't paying attention at the time—saw us march through the entrance hall and gave a short scream.

"Just find a goddamned wardrobe and hide in it!" Meridiana suggested as we worked our way up the stairs.

The house was a terrifying mixture of styles, once you paid attention to it. On the surface it seemed light and breezy, the sort of refined place you'd expect to find on the inside of all those nice, ivy-covered bricks. Once you started spotting the disturbing details, though, you found the personality of the owner crept through.

A row of oil paintings that ran up the stairs depicted everything from rape to infanticide, all rendered in the muted, soft brushstrokes you expect from old pictures. You can make anything look classy with a thin enough brush.

A bookcase at the head of the stairs was filled with volumes bound in something that still breathed, bookmarks shifting within the pages.

The flowers thrust into an ornate vase spat at me as I passed, their saliva thick and gelatinous.

A rug on the landing had obviously once tried to escape, the nails that held it fast also explaining the whimpering it offered as we walked past.

Out on the verandah we found things had moved on in our absence. A gang of maybe fifty or so people had made their way to the front of the house, all shouting and checking their guns.

The stables were on fire. Plumes of smoke billowed from the cracked windows. I thought about the row after row of human cattle Greaser had kept in there. As sickening a thought as it was, I hoped the fire would be a blessing. I was under no illusion they could have been saved, they were too far gone.

"My Agnes is in there!" Abernathy shouted. It took me a moment to realise he was referring to his ride. "She's carried me faithfully for ninety years or more, he'd better not let her burn to a crisp."

It was almost as if Lucifer had heard him as the stable doors crashed open and a herd of frightened rakh (and one nonplussed Agnes) came flooding out, trampling over the closest men.

So, yeah, the animals were safe, fuck the poor humans.

It took Greaser's men a few moments to respond, busily trying to get out of the way as the animals charged. Then they trained their guns on the open doorway, now filled with smoke, and begin to fire. Bullet after bullet ploughed into the smoke. After a few moments someone had the bright idea of actually waiting for a target. There was silence. And then a figure slowly walked into view. Lucifer, dragging Greaser behind him.

A few more shots rang out until a man—who had clearly decided he was leader in his employer's absence—told everyone to 'wait just a goddamned minute'.

Lucifer threw Greaser to the ground in front of him.

The man was still alive, though whether through the protection he'd previously bragged about or because Lucifer wanted him that way it was impossible to tell.

"Well then," my friend shouted, "if we're going to do it, then let's do it."

And the air filled with gunfire.

Whether the bullets from his opponent's guns found their mark or not, it was impossible to tell. If they did, it didn't bother Lucifer any. He just walked forward, emptying chamber after chamber into the men. While his six-shooters looked normal enough, they seemed to have a bottomless reservoir of bullets. He just fired and fired until his gun began to glow with the same heat that continued to radiate from his mouth.

It was a massacre, and one that didn't bother him a jot.

A thought occurred to me and I turned to Meridiana. "Isn't everyone immortal down here? How can you kill something that's immortal?"

"You can't," she said, "by definition. But you can destroy it for awhile. It depends on how powerful the being is that's being destroyed. Some things regrow. Some, like me or you for example, would just be lost. The little essence of life we have floating on the wind never again to gain form."

I looked at Agrat. "Well, thanks for that, I'm so glad you made me immortal!"

"Just try not to get destroyed," she replied. "As long as there's enough functioning meat left I'll still be able to cash you in one day."

"That's horrible."

"Something like him," Meridiana continued, pointing at Lucifer, "is almost too powerful to destroy at all. That's why he was banished in the first place. Kicked out and made Non Grata so that even if he did come back he wouldn't be able to achieve anything. Guess that's one plan that's gone to the wall."

"What does he want?" Biter asked me. "Has he told you? You're his friend, he must have told you?"

"He just said he wanted to come home. I don't think he has any big plan beyond that."

Agrat scoffed. "That's Lucifer, the one-time ruler of the Dominion of Circles and rival to the Almighty. Of course he's got a plan beyond that."

I suddenly realised there was silence. We looked down to see him staring up at us.

"She might be right at that," Lucifer said. "You all want to hear it?"

2.

WE DESCENDED INTO the charnel house that Greaser's garden had become. Everywhere you looked, someone lay in pieces. Dotted about, the rakh were nibbling on charred arms or legs. Nice animals.

Greaser was trying to threaten and cuss, pretty much a way of life from what I could tell of the man. Having Lucifer's boot on the back of his head, pushing his face down into the dirt, was cramping his style in that regard.

"I don't want to hear him right now," Lucifer said. "My ears are just about full. I'll listen presently though, because I am interested in all the things he has to say." Greaser whined and Lucifer pressed down with his boot. "Well, maybe not all the things."

Biter dropped down in front of him, bowing and scraping in the dirt. "O Lucifer!" he howled. "If I have done anything to offend you in your glorious munificence, anything at all, I can only ask that you forgive me. I didn't know! I couldn't have guessed! I mean... seriously, how the fuck was I supposed to know he wasn't just crazy? Huh? He looks crazy! He sounds crazy!" His tone was getting more and more panicked. "If he'd only said, 'I happen to be friends with the most wondrous Prince of Darkness, so mind your manners around me...' I would! Of course I would!"

"Get up, you ass," Lucifer said. "I'm far too old and out of the game for all that bowing and begging. Never was much my style anyway."

Biter slowly got back to his feet and shuffled behind the rest of us. "As you wish, my Lord," he muttered.

"Anyway," Lucifer continued, "ain't like Elwyn here knew, is it? When you're Non Grata there are rules. You can't so much as give your own damned name. Names have power, they open doors and start fights. I was nobody. Hell, still am."

"Please spare us the false humility," said Agrat. I was kind of surprised she knew the meaning of the word. "You said you were here with a plan?"

"I wasn't," he said. "I really wasn't. But I don't much like what I'm hearing about this little bastard and his friends in high places." He gave Greaser a little kick. "Things are not how they should be here. Maybe I shouldn't care but, damn it, I always did. That's why He kicked me out in the first place, I would keep questioning..."

"This isn't sounding much like a plan so far," said Agrat. "You've made me—indirectly, I might add, and certainly will if questioned—reverse the order and wish of the one being in existence whose orders and wishes are generally accepted as non-reversible. That's a big enemy

I just made; I'm hoping you're going to tell me why that shouldn't have me sobbing in fear."

Lucifer shrugged. "I doubt He'll be of a mind to punish anyone but me," he said, "and I'm happy to ride alone, you know that."

"Nah," side Biter. "Who would miss this?"

Lucifer shrugged. "Up to you. We rest up for a short while, then we ride on the Dominion of Clouds."

3

DOOMSDAY

CHAPTER TEN
GOD MADE THEM... I KILL THEM

1.

ALONZO SAT DOWN in his Observation Lounge and mentally shuffled the cards he had been dealt. The writer was in place, as was the Messiah and the Antichrist. This, he believed, would be the Holy Trinity moving forward. The wellspring from which a new, firmer, more potent and practical existence could be drawn. The people outside the town were becoming more afraid, more desperate by the moment, and that was also good. In his experience, nothing was so malleable as the mortal mind in a state of agitation. Never give them time to think. Just wind them up to their maximum capacity and then give them a vent, a way forward, a solution. And if some people lost their lives along the way, then that was no real problem. After all, who wouldn't rather give up all that hard work and uncertainty for an eternity reduced to spiritual essence?

"What you doing?" He looked up to see the small girl that was his current charge. She was pulling a wooden train along on a piece of string. Her bright, blonde pigtails gave her a wonderfully metaphorical halo as she stood in the doorway to the room.

"Keeping an eye on things," he replied.

"Sounds boring."

"You always think that, but someone's got to do it."

"Why? Just let them all do what they like."

Alonzo fought to control his temper. "That never ends well. Now leave me in peace so I can concentrate."

The little girl shrugged, dragged her wooden train over to the chair on the far side of the room, sat down and began to hum.

Alonzo did his best to ignore her, sweeping his arm over the floor and changing the scene playing out beneath him.

He found himself looking at a group of people riding hard through the hinterland between the Dominions. His eyes were drawn, most particularly, to the man at their centre.

"Oh, no," he sighed, "not him... why did he have to choose now to rear his head?"

"Someone you don't like?" asked the girl.

"Trouble," Alonzo replied. "Someone I didn't plan for."

He stamped his foot in anger, zooming in on the image and staring into Lucifer's face, writ large beneath him.

"You're supposed to be Non Grata!" he said. "So how am I looking at you?"

2.

WHEN LUCIFER HAD said we could rest up for a short while, I had kind of hoped it might be for more than ten minutes.

I hadn't slept now for over a day, and I was beginning to lose what little grip on reality I'd already possessed.

"We need to get to the Dominion of Clouds before the end of the Fastening," he said, by way of explanation. It left me none the wiser, but I was too tired and too confused to ask for more information. I knew I wouldn't understand it any better.

"I love how he just assumes I intend to ride with you." Agrat moaned. "As I haven't got better things to do with my time."

"If he's going up against the Dominion of Clouds," said Biter. "You want to be a part of it; don't deny it. You think anything else is going to be worth a damn while something like that's happening?"

"Perhaps I would be better placed talking to my friends there," she said, "rather than throwing myself in with outlaws."

"You haven't any friends there," said Lucifer, "never did."

This angered her so much I could only assume it was true.

"Well," said Biter, "as far as I can see, it's obvious. If something big is going down I want to be on the side that scares me most."

"He's not scary," I said. And I felt it, despite what I'd seen over the last half an hour. The old man had done nothing but watch my back ever since I'd met him. Ultimate evil my ass, he was alright by me.

"What do you know?" Biter said. "You're just a mortal."

"What about you?" I asked Meridiana. "You coming?"

"Biter has a point," she said. "Besides, I've stuck with the pair of you this far, I may as well see things through to the bitter end." She took my arm. "You've got to remember, not much happens to immortals like us, so even if it seems crazy it beats just another day in Hell."

"I've got everything I can loaded up," announced Abernathy, waddling out of the burned out stables. "Of course, you managed to set fire to most of my stock, but I'll let it slide in the interests of good customer relations."

"What about the people?" I asked. Of course, if I hadn't been such a squeamish coward I'd have gone in there and looked for myself.

"The what?" he asked.

"They're all gone," Lucifer said. "As quickly and as painlessly as I could make it."

That was some relief to my ailing conscience at least.

"And now," he said, "we're going to find out who he was working with."

He walked over to where Greaser was trussed up, tied to one of the statues by his pool.

My conscience began to wonder if it really was in the clear or not.

"You ready to talk?" Lucifer asked him.

"Fuck you," was the considered response.

"Now," Lucifer leaned casually on the statue, a splayed woman with a giant bladder, given the quantity of water she appeared to be producing. "You know who I am, yes? You've seen what I do. I'm not some rival entity. I'm the original. The enforcer. The Light Bearer. The One Who Burns. It's no lack of honour on your part to just tell me what I want to know."

Greaser smiled, a wet and bloody smile. "Let me put it another way, then: Fuck you, *old man*."

Lucifer shrugged. "Up to you. I reckon you'll be feeling a mite more communicative once we've been riding a while, though." He cut Greaser lose from the statue and dragged him over to where the rakh were waiting. I think he even whistled as he tied the man to a long length of rope dangling from the back of his saddle.

"Let's going," he said, climbing onto the animal's back and galloping out of the gate, Greaser dragged along behind in a cloud of dust and shouting.

Maybe he was a bit scary after all.

By the time we had descended the mountain and were once more outside Abernathy's store, Greaser was half the man he used to be. He'd lost a leg and an arm and had come to resemble an old potato that had been rolled in grit.

For the last few minutes he'd been screaming one word: "Alonzo."

"I'd thought as much," Lucifer replied, untying him. "But it's best to be sure before you start flinging accusations around."

He dragged what was left of the man over to edge of the marina and tossed him in. There was a scream and a loud splash, then he returned, clapping his hands together to knock off the dust.

Branches of Regret was still stood outside the store, arms wide, taking in the air.

"You were successful?" he asked as I walked over to him.

"Guess so," I replied. "We were able to lift a curse off my friend, and that was the main reason we went."

"Lucifer?"

"Yeah." I wasn't surprised he recognised him, clearly everyone did. "He's been with me all the time, but you wouldn't have been able to see him."

"I saw him."

"What? You could see him before? But nobody was supposed to be able to."

"I can't help that."

"Why didn't you say something?"

"I didn't think it was important. Are we going to the Dominion of Clouds to fight Alonzo now?"

"I don't know why you even bother to ask."

"Politeness."

"Yes, we are."

He nodded slowly. "It would be better were I to travel my own way, I think."

He slowly began to shrink into the earth at my feet, tendrils splitting off from his arms and legs as he pulled himself under. After a moment he was gone.

"Branches of Regret's going to meet us there," I said and went over to my rakh to sit in silence and be confused for a bit.

"Just give me a minute to lock up," said Abernathy. "I don't bother for short trips—the rats police things pretty well—but if we might be gone a while..."

Lucifer shook his head in despair. "Even the shopkeeper's coming?"

"I heard that, your munificent piece of shit!" Abernathy called, the sound of chains being dragged around inside the store. "Obviously I wouldn't give you any back chat, being so all powerful as you are. I'll do whatever you ask, even let you kiss my fat ass if that's what you're after. Because it sure sounds like that's what you're after..."

"I blame you," Lucifer said to me. "You attract them like flies."

"More the merrier! With Branches of Regret, there's seven of us!"

"Magnificent," he replied, with limited sincerity.

Eventually we were ready to leave, heading back out onto the road the way we'd come.

After a short while we veered away from the lake and towards the large cattle sheds I'd noticed earlier.

"I'm not sure I want to see inside there," I admitted as Lucifer drew to a halt a short distance away.

"You don't need to," he said. "We've seen all of Greaser's business we need to. This is just to send a quick message."

He climbed down and began to slowly walk towards the sheds. "You all stay back here."

The sheds stretched right across the field, row after row. The whole set up was more than twice the size of most of the towns I'd ridden through on my journey across America.

"I'm here to tell you something," Lucifer shouted. I was reminded of the time on our journey to Wormwood when he had spoken and I had heard the words clearly, regardless of distance, as if he had been speaking directly into my head rather than my ears. "Greaser is gone. Buzz is gone. This trade is gone."

I noticed a few people appearing at the entrances of the cattle sheds. Some were armed and ready for trouble, most were just confused.

"The Dominion of Circles is under my control again," Lucifer continued, "and I say you're done."

He raised his arms, tilted back his head and, with a roar, a ball of fire rose up from his throat and sailed into the air like a cannonball. Then another, and another...

The people that had appeared outside the cattle sheds weren't slow to run; still, most of them didn't make it. When the fireballs hit the roofs of the sheds, they erupted with a light and heat the like of which I'd never seen before. The entire place was ablaze. Huge columns of fire exploding like the heads of cabbages. The sky filled with flame and debris. Even back where we were, maybe quarter of a mile away, the heat was enough to have us holding our arms up in front of our faces, the rakh shifting nervously beneath us.

"I love him," said Biter in awe. "I ain't never loved a man before, but I love this one. I want to roll over and be his goddamned bitch."

"Stop talking," said Agrat. "Please... before I'm forced to vomit on you."

Lucifer turned back to us, slowly climbed onto his rakh and nodded. "That'll do," he said, and we cut away from the burning crater and on towards the Dominion of Clouds.

3.

HAVE YOU READ *the Bible?* he'd asked me.

Well, dear reader, I cannot claim to have done so, at least not in its entirety. I know it's terribly scurrilous to say so, but I always got rather bogged down in the endless lineages of David and the rules about what you could or could not do with goats.

I jest of course, but really, what a question! Well, no, not the question... the clear inference that lay behind it.

I really didn't know what to say.

I was being asked to write a sequel to the Good Book. Not something that had occurred to me as an option, within my career of rollicking adventures and questionable facts (and no, before you ask, I am not attempting sarcasm; I'm not what you would call a religious man, but I am not so bold—or stupid, given I was staring the sacred in the face—to mock such things).

He left me, confused and unable to comment, saying that we would discuss it more later.

The replica of my childhood home had begun to seem less charming as I became more disorientated and confused. As I had predicted earlier, with Billy and the good lady Forset, the sense of being a puppet dangling on a string was becoming more pronounced by the moment.

I stepped out of the library and found myself in a cloister of such gargantuan proportions that I felt unsteady on my feet for a few moments.

"Feel free to have a look around," Alonzo called, as he strode away. "Dinner will be served in an hour or so."

Dinner, yes... but served where? I would have to cross that bridge when I came to it.

I stood at the edge of the covered arcade, leaning back on a pillar fashioned—like everything else I could see—from white marble. It was so clean and perfect it didn't feel real. I touched it; the stone was cool and unblemished, it felt more like glass.

The quad was filled with a garden, neat and immaculate but still somehow possible to lose oneself in. I was reminded of pictures I had seen of Japanese gardens (despite the evidence of my story *Krahjira—King of Monsters*, I have never been there). A network of streams cut through the manicured grass, small wooden bridges crossing back and forth. Several pagodas stood between the trees, and at its centre was what I took to be a bandstand, a raised pearlescent structure surrounded by statues.

Idyllic but empty.

This was the same everywhere I went. I looked in through large windows into ornate halls, galleries and living spaces. Everywhere offered a genteel, beatific decadence, but no residents. As far as I could tell, Heaven was empty.

Once I had found the stairs, I descended to ground level and made my way into the garden.

I squatted down by the stream and dipped my fingers into the water; it was the same temperature as the air, and I could barely tell it was there. No fish swam in it. The stream was as devoid of inhabitants as everywhere else.

I sat down on a bench and tried to decide what to do with myself. As a writer, I felt it was important to try and explore the place; but it all felt somehow hollow, like the ceramic dainties that ladies like to buy for their mantels. A thing of crystalline beauty but surprisingly little soul. I began to suspect that everything was as false, as dreamed up for my benefit, as the library I had first found myself in.

Could I even be sure I was in Heaven at all? Or Hell? I would later come to understand they were movable concepts. Both had their physical geography, and yet both were also states of mind experienced by the dead mortals who passed into them. At that point, however, I was just a man lost by the side of a stream, wondering what ridiculous situation he had got himself into.

Perhaps more would be revealed at dinner.

As the time passed, I found myself becoming absurdly sleepy, lulled, I believe, by the soporific sound of the water and the general air of calm. I am not entirely sure if I slept or not. Possibly, the brief vision I experienced was a dream. I suspect such distinctions don't even matter.

A young girl walked across the grass towards me. She was dressed in the sort of white raiments that classical painters do so love to drape their celestial visions in. A jumble of Roman and Greek, shimmering togas and skin pale as milk. She pulled a toy train behind her on a piece of string.

"What are you doing?" she asked.

"Waiting," I replied. It seemed the only truthful answer.

She sat next to me on the bench. "Waiting's boring, isn't it?"

"Yes," I agreed, "though that depends on what you're waiting for. If you're waiting for something horrible, the time passes quickly enough, if you're waiting for something nice..."

"I don't like it. I just like things to happen."

"But then we wouldn't be able to enjoy them. If something was happening all the time, when do you get to relax and think about them? Appreciate them for what they are?"

She shrugged. "I suppose. I just get impatient."

"So do I, sometimes. Even more so when I was young like you."

She smiled. "Being young is nice. Nobody expects things from you."

"Oh, I don't know. You have to tidy your room, do your schoolwork. Do you play an instrument?" Most little girls I knew were forced by their parents to do so. Trudging their bored way along the keys of a piano or the strings of a violin.

"No. Do you think I should?"

"Up to you. I suppose it's nice to be able to make music. It takes a long time to get good at it, though, you need to be patient."

"Oh, I haven't got a lot of that."

"Patience?"

"Time. Never mind. I'm sure it wasn't important." She held up her little train and scrutinised it. "I like trains. They drag people around."

"And then you drag it around."

She smiled and nodded, then stood up and skipped away.

"Bye, then," I called after her, but she had vanished into the trees.

Later, either waking me from sleep or shaking me from my thoughts, a bobbing light, like a willow-the-wisp from a child's story book, appeared before me.

"And what are you?" I wondered.

It bobbed as if in reply and then slowly began to move away. I decided, in the absence of anything else to do, to follow it.

4.

THE SIEGE ON the Land Carriage was brief and seemingly unproductive.

Inside, keeping away from the windows, it was hard to decide whether the crowd had given up or been struck into guilty silence by a realisation of their own actions. Lord Forset was quick to expound such a theory, but then, with Billy's assistance, he had just carried the body of Brother Clement inside his cabin and the horror of that old, lifeless face hung heavy on him. The Order of Ruth, with the exception of Brother William, had retired to their cabins in order to pray. Billy suspected they would be hiding, more than talking to God, but that was fine, he didn't blame them. The rest of the party was now crammed into the front compartment, having decided it was better to stick together.

"Do you think they'll just leave us alone?" Forset wondered, the question aimed at nobody in particular.

"I think they're still angry," said Brother William, "and will want to lash out more before the day is done."

"It depends what happens, doesn't it?" asked Elisabeth. "If more people were let in to Wormwood, then they'd forget all about us."

"But they're not going to be, are they?" said Billy. "Be honest, it didn't make sense in the first place. 'We're going to do this a few at a time, because there are so many of you?' It's supposed to be the afterlife, not a riverboat."

Elisabeth couldn't help but nod. "It's just as Patrick said. We're puppets with our strings being tugged."

"I don't understand it," bemoaned her father. "This was supposed to be something beautiful. An amazing experience. Not this... horror."

She held his hand. "I'm sorry."

She had always suspected that his lifelong obsession with the miraculous Wormwood would end in disappointment. Not like this, of course; her expectation had simply been for an empty field and a gradual sense of disillusionment. This was much worse. To discover that the myth was real but then be cheated of fully exploring it. More than that: to be left with the inescapable impression that you had been had, that a greater plan was at work and its intentions were vaguely hostile. She knew he must be suffering a great deal.

The carriage shook again.

"Oh, God," said Forset, "they're back."

"I'm not sure," said Billy, "that didn't feel like people pressing at the outside."

The carriage shook again, and Billy was right. This wasn't an external pressure, they were rocking on their wheels.

"Someone's trying to get her started," said Forset, the idea somehow even worse to him that a simple attack.

This was his creation, his great invention; that it should be manhandled by these idiots...

The Land Carriage began to move.

5.

ALONZO STEPPED ALONG the shores of the Bristle lake like a crane hunting for food, constantly darting away from the lapping liquid so as not to ruin his boots.

After a few minutes he found what he was looking for. With a sigh, he removed his jacket and draped it over a rock. Then he rolled up his sleeve and grabbed at the thrashing torso at the lake's edge. He yanked it back onto the dry shore, letting it roll amongst the thick hairs that grew there. While the torso tried to right itself, fractured arms slapping against the soil as it tried to tip itself onto its back, Alonzo removed a handkerchief from his pocket and did his best to wipe his hand clean.

They both finished their tasks at the same time.

"Es oo es at?" said the torso, its mouth no longer functioning after its tongue had been wrenched out by one of the other residents of the lake.

"Yes, Greaser," Alonzo said, "it's me. You look well."

"Uck aff ant."

"Nothing would please me more than to do so, but first a little warning: did you tell them about me?"

The torso was silent.

"Yes, well, that probably answers my question, doesn't it?"

"O ice."

"There's always a choice, Greaser, just varying degrees of difficulty in making the right one."

"Reee."

"I'm sure you are." Alonzo looked at his mostly clean hand and sighed again. "Oh, well," he said. "One can't keep one's hands clean forever."

He reached down, grabbed Greaser's arm and pulled him back into the lake.

"O! O!" Greaser begged.

"Shush now," said Alonzo. "What's good for the goose is good for the gander; as a place of punitive contemplation, the mortals seem to love it."

Greaser bobbed back into the lake, pulled by many other hands, his shouting mouth choked off by the slopping tide.

Alonzo walked back up the shore and thought about what was likely to happen next.

6.

As WE RODE away from the Bristle, the after-effects of the last day or so weighing heavily on me, I found myself sinking lower and lower in my saddle, until eventually I must have fallen asleep.

I woke up later to find I was moving along at some speed, my rakh galloping across a wide field. The grass was a faint yellow. I squinted at it to try and make sure it wasn't hair, but we were moving so fast it was hard to tell.

"Elwyn's woken up!" Meridiana shouted, laughing.

Nobody else cared enough to comment.

I tried to sit up, but found that some considerate soul— let's be honest, it would have been Meridiana—had tied me to the saddle with my reins. I suppose I was glad of it; some sleep was better than none, and at least I hadn't fallen off and been trampled on. Now that I was awake, though,

I just felt trapped and stupid. It took some wriggling (and my rakh couldn't have made its disgust at my writhing around clearer had it written me a letter on the subject) but I eventually got myself loose and was able to sit up.

The terrain around us now was very different from the deep red gloom of the Bristle. The sky still held a stormy weight, but everything was much more open and light. I'd almost have called it pleasant if I wasn't being beaten up ass-wise and still in an utter state of confusion.

I wondered how long I'd slept. More to the point, how long did we still have to ride? I asked as much, but either nobody heard me above the sound of beating hooves or nobody could be bothered to answer.

The landscape was all but bare, the occasional dead tree throwing aggressive finger gestures at us as we passed. If the Bristle had been a place of constant horror, this was a region of absence, plain and empty, stretching on seemingly forever.

We stopped about five minutes later, giving me a chance to climb off and do a proper job of untangling myself and straightening my clothes.

"You were like a baby," said Biter, "riding along on its mother's back."

This amused him so greatly I decided to be nice and not punch him in the face.

"How far have we got to go?" I asked.

"Another couple of hours should do it," said Lucifer, staring out towards the horizon, at absolutely fuck all, as far as I could tell.

"You don't drag your heels when he's by your side," said Biter, offering the old man his usual doe-eyed look. "We've been flying!"

"Literally?" I had visions of waking up in free fall.

"Well, no, but we've been riding real fast. We passed through the Archimedes Belt in, like, twenty minutes!"

"Good." I wasn't going to ask, I'd sit down and nod at a map one day, should all this pan out fine. "You think they know we're coming?"

"Of course they do," said Agrat. Her mood, as far as I could tell, was getting even worse, the closer we got to the Dominion of Clouds. "Omnipotence is hard to beat, you silly little man."

"Alonzo's not omnipotent," said Lucifer. "And, in my experience, the Boss was only ever as omnipotent as He could be bothered to be. Being able to know everything is fine, caring enough to do so is another matter."

"You two obviously got on real well," I said, the ramification of that slowly starting to sink in. Maybe I could see why Agrat was so foul-tempered; how stupid did you have to be to pick a fight with the supreme being?

"I loved Him," said Lucifer, "but I don't believe the feeling was reciprocated."

Those of us that needed it took a few mouthfuls of water, then we got back in the saddle and continued on our way.

7.

"WE'RE GOING PAST Wormwood," said Brother William, leaning out of the window.

"Get your head back inside," said Elisabeth, "before someone tries to shoot it off."

"I don't think there's much risk of that now," said her father. "They're happy to ignore us back here, now they have control of the engine."

They had left the camp behind and the view out of the windows was of the empty plain in front of Wormwood.

"But why steal it in the first place?" wondered Billy. "You wouldn't think they'd want to just high-tail it out of here, not while there was still a chance of their getting into Wormwood."

"At least it's got us clear, too," said Elisabeth. "If we can take back control of the engine, we're in a much safer position than we were."

"Yeah," said Billy. "Take back control of the engine. Because that won't be difficult at all, will it?"

"It depends what they have in mind," said Lord Forset. "As you say, I can't believe they're planning on just driving off, so they'll likely stop soon; and we need to be ready to fight them off when they do."

8.

SCOTT CLAREMONT FELT better than he had in days. The air rushing past his face had beaten away his hangover and he was back in control of his own destiny again. It had been some time since he'd worked the rails for a living. When he'd first left home, he'd signed up with the Houston and Texas Central Railway. He'd looked at those heavy metal tracks in the dirt and thought: *That's it, that's the way out of here.*

Even though he'd run the same route for a couple of years, first as a boiler-man then as the engineer, always returning back to the station from which he'd left, the train had represented freedom to him like nothing before. To ride that great, iron beast towards the horizon, wondering if one day you'd just break free of the tracks and keep going. It was one hell of a feeling.

The Land Carriage was a dream come true, all the power without the tracks. He could, indeed, go wherever he wanted. He could stoke that fire and roar through the dirt.

He had worried for a moment that the controls would be unfamiliar, but it had been the work of a few minutes to get the engine rolling. The engineer had kept the boiler lit, no doubt using it to power the other facilities back there, lights and such, so all he'd had to do was stoke it up and let her rip.

He looked around for a whistle, wanting to shout to the world that he was on his way. He pulled the chain, laughing at the high, piercing note that soared through the air.

He looked at Wormwood as he drove past, snatched glimpses of its empty streets and buildings.

"I came a long way to see you," he shouted, "and I'm damned if I'm going to be kept waiting any longer!"

He laughed again, pushing forward into the desert beyond the town, wanting to put a decent chunk of distance between them.

It had taken him a short while to get the hang of the directional controls. When you were on the tracks you only needed forward and back. But now he was in the open, he found the measure of them, carving out a wide curve so that, after ten minutes or so, he was facing back towards the town.

"Last stop, the ever-after!" he shouted, pulling on the whistle again. He began to stoke the boiler even higher, piling on the pressure. When he hit Wormwood, he wanted to be going as fast and as heavy as possible.

*   *   *

9.

THE FLOATING ORB led me out of the garden on the other side of the quad. The arcade was identical, and I walked past more empty rooms and blank spaces as I trailed along after my ethereal host.

"Is dinner served, perchance?" I asked it. I didn't expect a reply and it failed to surprise me, simply floating a few feet ahead, casting its faint, amber light on the blank white walls and pillars.

We ascended a set of stairs which opened out into a huge hall. Like everything else, it was blank, white and featureless, and at the far end of the cavernous space sat a table, ornately laid and featuring guests.

"Well thank the Lord for that," I said. "I was beginning to think there was nobody else in this entire place but me."

To the left was a well-dressed gentleman who would have cut a dapper figure were it not for his face. He had a blank patch of skin where his eyes should be. He barely acknowledged my arrival; I forgave him for not looking up, of course, but he might have said hello.

Across the table from the surly fellow was a far more congenial couple. A beautiful young girl of negroid descent and, well, my first assumption was that I was dining in high company indeed...

"Oh," I said, on spotting him... "You're not..." I wondered if I should bow.

"His name's Soldier Joe," said the girl. "Don't let the beard and hair fool you, he's as much a stranger around here as you are."

"My name's not actually Joe," the man admitted, "though for the moment I can't rightly remember what it is, so I suppose it'll do for now."

This was shaping up to be like every publishing dinner I'd ever known: a table filled with the aggressive, the beautiful and the mad.

"Well, as a man who has had his own surfeit of names, I can understand the confusion," I said. "I'm Patrick Irish, but up until recently I wrote under the name of Roderick Quartershaft."

This provoked a veritable slab of indifference. Clearly I was not in the company of devotees.

"I've not been much of a reader," said Soldier Joe. "Up until very recently I've had... a number of health problems."

"Please," I lied, "it hardly matters! Not everyone's a reader, after all. How about..." I looked to the other gentleman and immediately shut my terribly stupid mouth.

"I never seem to find the time," he said and smiled. It wasn't a pleasant smile. Rather a sharp, hostile thing. The kind of smile a man offers you so that you know that, while he is aware of your insult, he is far too scary and violent to let it upset him. Though he is probably going to kill you anyway. I couldn't think of anything to say that might make matters better, so I just shut up for all of ten seconds and then changed the subject.

"And your name?" I asked the girl.

"Hope Lane," she replied.

"Lovely. Like an address. To a particularly wonderful house."

Oh, Irish, you were not at your best. She was polite enough to laugh.

"Well," I said, "this is all very nice, isn't it?"

I'm English, you see. We like to deal in intangible conversations for as long as possible.

"Nice?" the blind gentleman asked. I supposed I should have asked him his name too, but I was avoiding any contact unless under direct force.

"Well," I said, sitting down as far away from him as was possible, given the limited space available. "You know... erm... dinner in Heaven. I've been in worse situations. Especially of late. Did you all travel to Wormwood like me?"

I intentionally looked to the other couple, hoping they'd answer. They took pity on me.

"We all came together, actually." Hope said.

"Though I don't really remember it," admitted Soldier Joe.

"And most of my friends, and the woman I loved more than life itself, died on the way," announced the blind man.

Much more of this, I thought, and I would have no other choice but to impale myself on a fish knife.

"That's awful," I said.

"Henry Jones," he replied. It took me a moment to understand the significance of the two words. Eventually I realised he was offering his name.

"Ah, right. Good to meet you, Mr Jones."

"You ain't heard of me?"

"No... I don't think so." I smiled awkwardly and then realised he couldn't see it, so it didn't help.

"Oh," he replied. "Most have."

"The burden of fame, I know it well. My books have sold so well that..."

"I killed a lot of people in my time."

"Ah. Right, you're that sort of famous. I see. Lovely. Probably better, actually, I imagine you're rarely troubled for autographs and the such." I looked around, desperate for someone to mention the arrival of soup.

"I've signed many," he replied, forming a pretend gun with his fingers and miming a shot in my direction.

I was saved the need to faint or hide under the table by the arrival of Alonzo.

"My friends!" he called, walking through the empty hall towards us. "So sorry to have kept you waiting. It's all work, work, work for me at the moment."

Whether I trusted the man or not, he drew the focus of a room and I was so relieved to have it taken from me I could have kissed him. Following in his wake was the young girl I'd dreamed about earlier. Or not. For all I knew I was dreaming the meal too. It had all got a little confused by that point.

It suddenly occurred to me that it might be a bit of a squeeze at the table for another two, yet, even as I thought it, I looked down and found the table had expanded. I wasn't aware of it having done so, it was simply as if it had always been that size.

"I trust you slept well?" Alonzo asked Soldier Joe and Hope.

"Our heads were kind of busy," Soldier Joe replied. "Speaking for myself, I've slept so long I can skip a night here or there."

"You've been here longer than me, then?" I asked. I had assumed they had been vanished from the camp at the same time as I.

"I'm afraid," explained Alonzo, "I have had to indulge in some gentle manipulation, where time is concerned. Unlike my patron, I have not the blessing of omnipresence. I therefore have found myself spread somewhat thin over the last day or so."

He sat down facing me, whipping his white napkin from the place in front of him and draping it across his lap.

"Such is the curse of one who wishes to get things done," he added. "Long days and nights."

The little girl pulled herself onto the last empty chair, placing her toy train between her knife and fork. I looked at it and noticed, for the first time, what a startling similarity it bore to Lord Forset's Land Carriage.

"You like trains, I think? I travelled here in something rather like one."

"They're a means to an end," she said, in a rather adult tone.

10.

"WE'RE TURNING BACK on ourselves!" Billy announced. "Heading right back towards Wormwood. At a hell of a pace, too."

"Oh, Lord," said Elisabeth. "You don't think he means to..."

"Smash his way in?" Brother William interrupted.

"He can't!" Lord Forset said, his face blanching at the thought.

"You never know," said Billy. "He might make a dent."

"You don't understand," Forset replied. "My equipment, the stores on the back. The power unit for the Forset Thunderpack alone is likely to level half the valley if it ignites."

"We've been travelling around with that kind of cargo and you didn't tell me?"

"I'm pretty sure I mentioned the Thunderpack was capable of extreme damage if it was in operation for too long."

Billy waved his hands in the air, exasperated. "Yes, probably, but it slipped my mind, what with recent events. Besides, you have a tendency to..."

"What? Are you accusing me of exaggeration? I am a scientist, sir! Whatever I say can be taken as nothing less than the simple, unvarnished truth!"

"Stop arguing, the pair of you," insisted Elisabeth. "It's hardly helping."

"Fine," agreed Billy. "I just wished I'd known to be a bit more careful when I was driving this thing full pelt through uneven terrain."

"It's stable enough in normal circumstances," said Forset. "I didn't anticipate a situation where someone might consider driving the Land Carriage at full speed towards a solid object."

"We've got to get control of the engine," Elisabeth said. "Get up there and deal with him."

The Land Carriage jolted as it picked up speed, forcing them to steady themselves against the walls of the carriage.

"And quickly," Billy agreed. "At this rate we'll be nothing but scrap and splinters in a matter of minutes."

Lord Forset checked his rifle. "We can work our way through the carriages, but we're likely to be stuck in a bottleneck when we get to the end, if he's armed..."

"And he's bound to be," added Elisabeth.

"Then we have the problem of how we get through the final adjoining door without his taking pot shots at us," her father continued.

"I might have an idea about that," his daughter said.

11.

THE OPEN PLAIN had given way to mountains. This place just loved mountains, I decided, and it did them so well. Great, towering, evil looking things they were. The sort of rocky outcrops that looked like they were stabbing the sky right in its guts.

"Nearly there," shouted Meridiana, who had been riding alongside me for the last stretch. "I came this far once, when I was a kid. Just to take a look at how the other half lived."

The trail opened out onto a plateau that looked out onto nothing but fresh air. Lucifer stopped his rakh and dismounted, walking up to the edge and gazing into the thin, white mist ahead.

I joined him, trying to see anything ahead, a shadow of another mountain, or the faint outline of the ground below. There was nothing, just mist and clouds.

"Here we are," he said. "The entrance to the Dominion of Clouds."

"I kind of assumed the name was... what was that word you used before? A meatavore."

"Metaphor. And it doesn't mean quite what you think it does."

"Ah, what does these days? So the place is really built out of clouds, huh?"

"No. This is just the gateway."

"Which we need to cross somehow?"

"Yes."

"Any idea how?"

"No."

"Great."

I walked the edge of the plateau, not because I had an idea, but because I didn't.

As I turned to head back, a small, unhealthy looking bush growing out of the rock began to grow larger. It became healthier, greener, its leaves more dense. Then it dropped forward and seemed to pour itself onto the ground in front of me.

Branches of Regret.

"Hi, Branches," I said, as he took his normal shape. "You missed a fun ride."

"I was communing with my brothers," he said.

"Of course you were. We're now looking at the road ahead and figuring it might be a bit harder to travel than we'd hoped."

He walked to the edge. "This is not a problem," he said. "All you need is a bridge."

With that he stamped his feet, fine roots erupting from between his toes and embedded themselves in the cracks in the rock. He reached his arms up into the air and began to stretch, and stretch, and stretch...

He toppled forward, his body creaking and groaning as it grew wider and longer, vanishing out into the mist. After a moment there came a noise in the distance, like a tree falling over.

Slowly, he settled, flattening out, filling in the gaps. Eventually we were looking at what—if you had no qualms about riding over someone you'd had a conversation with—you could call a bridge.

"See?" I said to anyone that would listen. "How could you not like him?"

"Please move quickly," came a voice through the clouds, his normal, deep tone now strained and reedy. "This is not as easy as it may look."

"And it looked real easy," said Biter.

We climbed back in our saddles and rode across Branches of Regret's back. Every now and then there was a creak or groan from beneath us. At one nerve-wracking point there was even the sound of splintering.

"Quickly now," he said, his voice more strained than ever. "I would be saddened were I forced to drop you all into the infinite chasm between one Dominion and another."

I decided I would be saddened too and swore at my rakh until the useless piece of shit found a bit more speed.

There was nothing to see on either side of us, just the same white mists. We weren't even sure we'd arrived until the air filled with the sound of creaking wood and Branches of Regret appeared next to us, his face looking as impassive as ever, despite what he'd just been through.

"You are safely across," he announced. "I suggest we travel the last short distance together."

We all slowed our rakh to a trot and pushed through the mist in silence.

I guess Lucifer knew what was ahead, but it was obvious the others didn't. For all Agrat's pretensions and history, she had never stepped out of the Dominion of Circles. These were Hell's children, and what we don't know, or struggle to relate to, is what scares us most.

Slowly—barely noticeable to begin with, just shadows in the fog—shapes began to form. Huge towers, lights pulsing at the top of them, like lighthouses warning lost souls not to crash into Heaven's shore. Then the building—the citadel, as Lucifer called it. To call it a building is to suggest it was limited in size. Buildings are what humans make when they want to shove themselves into a manageable box. It's our way of breaking up the huge spaces that make us feel so small by creating smaller ones we can fill out easier. The architects of Heaven had no such fears. The citadel was bigger than anything I can try and compare it to. I could say it was the size of a city, but that would be to shrink it. The size of a country? Maybe. Though how do you fit an idea like that in your head? That was my problem, I think, looking up at its white walls, filled with regular lit windows stretching as far as I could see: I couldn't make the place fit in my head.

For all its size, it was incredibly plain. Straight lines and no ornamentation. White walls, untarnished. It looked like something your mom would beat you for touching. Perfect. Clean. Huge.

Yep. That about sums it up. Heaven. Big, clean and intimidating.

"That don't seem like the sort of place you'd come from," I said to Lucifer. "They put sheets down on the floors in case you tracked dirt in?"

"It was a long time ago," he said. "We've all changed."

There was nothing so obvious or welcoming as a door or gate. Lucifer just came to a halt in front of one patch of blank white wall that looked much the same as any other.

"It's strange," he said, looking around. "For all its austerity, the citadel is always buzzing with life. You could feel it, even on the outside; the energy of all the souls inside. This is... dead, empty... hollow."

He looked up at the wall.

"Alonzo! Either come out or let me in, I don't intend to stand here for eternity."

That's it, I thought, let's start on the right foot why don't we?

12.

I HAD WISHED for soup but I got fish. I suppose, from what I can remember of my Sunday School lessons, it is a notoriously holy dish.

Jones was clearly no more in the mood for dining than he was polite conversation.

"Enough of this," he said, pushing his plate to one side. "Why are we all sat here like it's a goddamned party? You brought us here for a reason and I want to know more."

"You know my offer, old friend," said Alonzo, "The governing of the Dominion of Circles, or Hell, if you must. I don't think I can put it any clearer."

"You want him to run Hell?" asked Hope Lane.

"Problem with that?" Jones replied with a sneer.

She stared at her fish, a bloated, glistening thing with skin like mercury. "I'm sure you're ideally suited to the job."

"Precisely!" Alonzo said. "That's the thing! You're all perfect for the roles I have in mind for you. A brave new start, learning lessons from the past and forging a better, controlled, future."

"It is rather hard to swallow," I said. "Maybe it's because we're just simple, mortal folk, but I can't say I'm clear on things either. You say you want a new Bible?"

"Yes! The old one is far too conflicted. Full of mixed messages, confusing imagery and contradictions. People don't know what to believe! Should they turn the other cheek or stone those who trespass against them? Are you sinners or are you incapable of sin because you're God's creatures? Does God forgive or does he condemn? Does he tempt or does he not? Is God loving or brutal?"

"Or both?" I suggested.

"Precisely!" Alonzo removed the skin from his fish with once perfect sweep of his knife. "That's exactly the problem! The damn thing can't even agree how many apostles there were! This is what happens when you let a mortal edit... Especially as a group. Mortals can't handle complexity. They don't deal with nuance. You've proved as much for two thousand years, fighting each other over interpretation, symbology... We need to start again. Clear messages." He looked to Soldier Joe and Jones in turn. "Clear heroes and villains. The sort of thing your lot can handle and work with. Then, perhaps, we can get everything back on an even keel."

"Which begs the question," said Jones, "who the hell are you to be doing such a thing?"

"I'm the last authority," Alonzo sighed. "The one left holding the pieces."

"Well," said Soldier Joe, "I'll ask, as everybody else is pussyfooting around it. Where's God?"

Alonzo sighed. "Lost in his own disinterest as usual, I'm afraid. Ever since he created you, he has grown more and more obsessed with mortality. He says it's the key to enlightenment, if you can believe such a thing! That you can never truly know the point of it all unless you're in a position to lose it. Utter guff, both philosophically and theologically, in my opinion. If God doesn't know the meaning of existence, then there simply isn't one. But he will have his little games and experiments."

"Games are fun," said the little girl, looking suspiciously at her fish, as if it might come back to life and bite her on the finger. "They're the best."

"Oh, just eat your food!" Alonzo snapped. "What does it matter about God anyway? You don't usually check for his approval whenever you do anything, which is rather my point. The important thing is: I'm doing what's best."

"I'm sorry," I said, "but that's still not enough for me. You're talking as if we can just wipe out the entire history of a religion and start again!"

"Of course we can. Mortals like to do as they're told. All you have to do is tell them loudly and clearly."

"But what about all the other religions in the world? Hinduism? Buddhism? Islam?"

"They're not my problem. Besides, if we do this right, then we'll put a stop to all that too. Confusion, chaos and disagreements. It's no good. We need one, clear, defined path."

"Free will?"

"Since when did that get you anywhere? Combine the right infrastructure with something suitably attention-grabbing. We'll have the world's attention, and from that we can build."

"Attention-grabbing? Like what?"

He waved the question away. "I don't want to talk about that, I take no pleasure in it, but the sacrifice will be all to the good."

Hope was shaking her head. "Sacrifice?"

"Of course, as much as I find it distasteful, there's nothing mortals respond to better than a bit of death."

13.

"SHE'LL BE COMING round the mountain when she comes!" Claremont sang, his voice carrying over the roar of the boiler as he pushed the Land Carriage faster and faster towards Wormwood. "She'll be coming round the mountain when she comes! She'll be coming round the mountain, coming round the mountain, coming round the mountain when she comes!"

In the distance, the beautiful, perfect town grew larger and larger, sat at the centre of a tunnel of dust and smoke kicked up by the Land Carriage as it tore across the open plain.

* * *

14.

BILLY, FORSET AND Brother William were gathered behind the door that led to the engine.

"He's locked it," said Billy, kicking at the door in disgust.

"Why would you design the door so it could be locked from the engine side?" asked Brother William.

"I thought it was a good security measure in case we were boarded," admitted Forset with some embarrassment.

"We could try and break it down?" Billy suggested. "Though if there's a better way of warning him we're coming, I can't think of it."

"He must know we're coming anyway," said Brother William. "He knows we're onboard. In fact he's probably wondering what's taking us so long to try something."

"We'll have to cross the roof," said Billy, moving back to the other end of the dining carriage. "Climb up on this side and make our way along."

"At this speed?" Brother William was clearly unimpressed by the thought.

"Unless you have a better idea, I can't see another way of getting at him." Billy admitted.

"He's right," said Forset. "And if we're going to do it, we need to get on with it."

Billy opened the door and they stepped out onto the gangway between the carriages. "I'll go first," he said, looking at Brother William. "Give me a foot up and then pass me my rifle when I'm up there." The novice nodded.

The dust that encircled them made it hard to breathe and almost impossible to see as Billy put his foot in Brother William's cupped hands and launched himself upward. He grabbed the edge of the carriage roof and, pushing against the slipstream of air that roared against him, dragged himself up so he was lying flat on his belly. He slowly revolved his body so he was looking back down at them, keeping one hand gripped tightly on the roof as he reached down for the offered rifle.

Turning back towards the engine, he began to crawl forwards. Following his example, the others climbed up after him.

15.

As DINNER PARTIES went, I had attended better. A wise man always tries to avoid discussing religion at the dining table, and we could hardly avoid it.

"Unbelievable!" Hope shouted. "So your glorious new future is built on the back of murder?"

"I'd hardly call it murder," said Alonzo, refusing to let his temper match hers. "More an unfortunate accident."

"One that you have engineered," I reminded him.

"Slightly encouraged."

"Close enough."

He put down his knife and fork, resolutely trying to remain calm. "If there's one thing your history has proven, it's that it takes spilled blood to get your attention. Perhaps you ought to ask yourselves why that is before criticising me."

"Blame God," said Jones. "That usually works for me."

"You'll have to find Him first," sighed Alonzo. Then, in a burst of energy, he swept his arm across the table and sent a wave of crockery and cutlery flying. Those strange white walls were finally decorated, with the splattered remains of our food.

"Why do you all have to make it so difficult?" he asked. "All I want to do is get things organised. To establish a nice, calm, ordered world rather than the messy, bloody, screaming, filthy, pitiful, desperate... *thing* you all insist on inhabiting."

He settled back in his chair. "I'm trying to help."

"Alonzo!" a voice shouted, from where we couldn't tell. "Either come out or let me in, I don't intend to stand here for eternity."

"Fine!" he said, jumping to his feet. "Do what you like. Why should I care? I wash my hands of the lot of you."

He began to march out of the hall before turning around and pointing his finger at the young girl. "And as for you... Grow up! Take some responsibility! I'm sick of tidying up after your messes. Two choices, either take over again or—if you insist on playing at being mortal—do the job properly and have the decency to die!"

With that he stormed out.

We wouldn't see him again.

16.

BILLY INCHED CLOSER and closer to the front of the carriage, his rifle held underneath him.

When he lifted his head, he could see Wormwood growing larger before them. He reckoned they had maybe two minutes before it would be too late for him to do anything anyway. The Land Carriage couldn't brake quickly, nor could it take a steep course correction at this speed. If he wanted to achieve either, he would need to do it gradually, and that meant he needed to get hold of the controls now.

As he approached the edge of the carriage, he became aware of sound of singing from below.

"We'll all be singin' hallelujah when she comes! We'll all be singin' hallelujah when she comes! We'll all be singin' hallelujah, singing hallelujah, singing hallelujah when she comes!"

Billy had no mind to sing 'hallelujah' or anything else in the current situation.

He pulled his rifle out from beneath him. The rogue driver had his back to him, so if he were quick he could end this in a matter of moments. As he raised the rifle, he noticed his shadow falling across the cabin. Claremont noticed it too.

The man spun around, revolver in hand, still singing his happy refrain as he fired two shots into the edge of the roof.

Billy's face filled with splinters as he instinctively rolled back, trying to get out of range. He felt his boot connect with Forset behind him, and then he was tumbling. The rifle fell from his grip and the wind caught him as he fell over the side.

17.

"Yes?" Alonzo asked, as if we weren't nothing more than a gang of Bible salesmen.

He had appeared to walk right through the plain white wall in front of us, the stone parting like a curtain to let him out, shrinking back the moment he passed. I recognised him, of course, from when he had been cock of the walk, talking to everyone after the town had first appeared. He'd lost some of that gloss now, for sure. He looked tired, pissed off, as if he wanted to be anywhere but here.

"Alonzo," said Lucifer, stepping down from his rakh. "I would have words."

"Of course you would," Alonzo answered with a sigh. "And I'd love to catch up, normally, but it's a trying time and I really don't have the patience for it right now."

"You'll have to find some." Lucifer continued to stare up at the citadel. "It's empty."

"For the most part," Alonzo agreed. "Has been for years. These are not good times for the Dominion of Clouds, old friend."

"Where did everyone go?"

"Elsewhere... I don't know. Dominion of Circles, the mortal world... there's been no control here for eons." He looked pleadingly at Lucifer. "You know what He was like? He got worse. People despaired. They knew a sinking ship when they saw one. So people left: one by one, then great caravans of them."

"But the mortal souls?"

"Few and far between, these days. They all seem to end up in the Dominion of Circles, obsessed with their sins and determined to atone. Either that or they don't believe in us at all. It's not like it used to be. Things have got confused. *They've* got confused. That's why I've been doing all this, trying to pull things together again. You could help?"

"You've been trading in souls with a man called Greaser." Lucifer looked down at the ground. "Pulling in mortals, that right?"

Alonzo looked angry now. "I did whatever I had to to keep everything going! You know how it works as well as I do. Thanks to His infinite wisdom, we need the temporaries for our power, we need their belief, their stupid, butterfly minds. I had to make allegiances with people I wouldn't normally consort with. I needed power."

"Ain't the way to do it."

"Fine!" Alonzo shouted. "You too, eh? Nobody's willing to get their hands a little dirty in order to fix the problem but me?" His hand dropped to his belt, to his holster. "Then you can all just do as you're told for once!"

The shot rang out before any of us had even seen the gun.

18.

"I've GOT YOU!" Forset shouted, his hands digging in to Billy's boot, desperate to maintain their grip. Brother William had a firm hold on Forset's legs, the weight of the two of them enough to compensate for Billy as he hung backwards over the edge of the carriage.

"You've got to stop him!" Billy shouted. "To hell with me! Put that bastard down before we're all done for!"

The whine of the Forset Thunderpack cut through the sound of the Land Carriage as Elisabeth came flying past him. Her hair streaked straight back from her head as she arced down towards the engine and Claremont, revolver in her hand.

Her target had a moment to look shocked at this speeding angel before she put a bullet in him and he toppled back against the controls. Another shot and he slumped forward, hitting the deck.

Elisabeth swerved around, returning for Billy.

"Quickly!" she shouted. "I've only got a few more seconds before I have to cut the power."

She grabbed onto him, the pair of them awkwardly upside down to each other like a royal playing card taking flight.

"Let go!" she shouted to her father, pulling back up, the strength of the rockets bringing Billy with her as she gave one last push towards the cabin.

There was little grace in their landing, colliding with the side of the cab. Billy dropped on top of Claremont's body as Elisabeth fought to cut the power on the Thunderpack, as its terrifying whine threatened to deafen them both.

Billy was straight on his feet, applying the brake. Slowly at first, so the whole vehicle didn't jackknife. Then he reached for the steering column, riding both at the same time, slowing their speed and angling them to the left.

"It's going to be close," he said, straining against the levers. "So close."

Behind them, Forset and Brother William slowly descended into the cab.

"Oh, my dear!" Forset laughed, taking hold of his daughter. "You're a marvel!"

The levers were fighting Billy, desperate to tear out of his grip. He felt like he was wrestling the entire vehicle.

Wormwood towered before them, even as they veered towards its far side.

There was a terrifying *crack* as the Land Carriage clipped whatever invisible barrier it was that had kept them from entering, the whole train rattling along the curve, threatening to topple but carried forward by its own momentum.

Ahead of them, crowds of people ran for cover, but there was no need. Finally, mercifully, the Land Carriage came to a halt.

*   *   *

19.

ALONZO STUMBLED BACKWARDS, Lucifer's bullet having hit him square in the chest.

His hand twitched once more towards his belt and Lucifer fired again, two shots in quick succession.

"Don't make me do it," the old man said. "You're a powerful man, Alonzo but if anyone can kill you..."

"It's you!" Alonzo spat, dropping to his knees but still digging for his gun.

One last shot. Alonzo toppled sideways, coming to rest like a man in his bed, drawing his knees up for comfort.

Lucifer towered over him. "We were just talking," he said. "It didn't have to come to this. I just wanted to know."

"You'll figure it all out," said Alonzo. "My aim was true."

"You didn't get off a shot."

Alonzo rolled onto his back, his coat flapping open. There was no gun in his holster.

"You think?" he said.

And from somewhere far away we heard the sound of a gun fire and the world turned on its head.

20.

"BLAME GOD," JONES said again.

We had sat in silence for a moment after Alonzo had left, none of us capable of filling the absurd void his conversation had left us with. The concepts he had discussed, the notions he had offered, they were too big for any of us to get our heads around.

"I'm sorry?" I asked him.

"When I first met Alonzo," Jones continued, "I was working in a freakshow. Living day by day with people gawking at me, pawing at me, treating me like shit."

"I'm sorry," I said, and for all his charmlessness I meant it.

"He told me of a place where you could walk right into Heaven. Stroll on in and chew the fat with God. I told him then that the only things I wanted to say to Him weren't pretty. When you've lived a life like I have you don't pray much. You don't have anything to be grateful for.

"No. That's not true. There was one thing. Harmonium. My wife. The one good thing in my life. She helped me find this place. Always by my side. Then I lost her. And I have to think... I have to consider... who exactly is to blame for all that? I thought I'd find her here. Dead, maybe, but I didn't care about that. I'd die too if that's what it took to be with her again. No problem. But she isn't here. I'm still without her. And I wonder to myself... who's to blame for that?"

"Blame God," said the little girl, pushing her wooden train along the table cloth.

"Exactly," said Jones. "Exactly that. Yes. Blame God." He looked right at her. "Only God's not in his right mind, is He? He's playing another game. He's pretending to be one of us. A little, living, breathing mortal. Because He wants to see how we live."

"And how you die," she added, sitting back in her chair, a bored look on her face.

"Yeah," he agreed, "how we die. I'm thinking that might just be the message I always wanted to pass on to God when I met Him."

He stood up, pulled out his pistol and pointed it at the little girl. The table erupted in panic.

She turned to look at me. "Told you I didn't have time to learn the piano," she said.

And Henry Jones shot God right in the head.

ABOUT THE AUTHOR

GUY ADAMS IS a no-good, pen-toting son of a bitch. Responsible for over twenty penny-dreadfuls and scientific romances such as *The World House* and the *Deadbeat* series. He has also worked with the Hammer Books Gang creating novelisations of their foul kinematographs and has been known to operate under the alias of John Watson M.D. writing novels featuring that pansy-ass detective Sherlock Holmes. He is wanted in several states and a reward is offered for anyone quick enough to slip a noose around his crooked neck. Further evidence of his crimes can be found on his Wild Western Waystation:

www.guyadamsauthor.com

BLOOD
AND
FEATHERS
LOU MORGAN

'A hell of a ride, but heaven to read: eerie, compelling and very funny.'
MICHAEL MARSHALL SMITH

UK ISBN: 978-1-78108-018-4 • US ISBN: 978-1-78108-019-1 • £7.99/$9.99

Alice isn't having the best of days - late for work, missed her bus, and now she's getting rained on - but it's about to get worse. The war between the angels and the Fallen is escalating and innocent civilians are getting caught in the cross-fire. If the balance is to be restored, the angels must act - or risk the Fallen taking control. Forever. That's where Alice comes in. Hunted by the Fallen and guided by Mallory - a disgraced angel with a drinking problem he doesn't want to fix - Alice will learn the truth about her own history... and why the angels want to send her to hell. What do the Fallen want from her? How does Mallory know so much about her past? What is it the angels are hiding - and can she trust either side?

UK ISBN: 978-1-78108-122-8 • US ISBN: 978-1-78108-123-5 • £7.99/$9.99 CAN $12.99

Driven out of hell and with nothing to lose, the Fallen wage open warfare against the angels on the streets. And they're winning. As the balance tips towards the darkness, Alice — barely recovered from her own ordeal in hell and struggling to start over — once again finds herself in the eye of the storm. But with the chaos spreading and the Archangel Michael determined to destroy Lucifer whatever the cost, is the price simply too high? And what sacrifices will Alice and the angels have to make in order to pay it? The Fallen will rise. Trust will be betrayed. And all hell breaks loose...

'Steve Rasnic Tem is a rare treasure'
NYT Bestselling Author Dan Simmons

DEADFALL HOTEL

STEVE RASNIC TEM

UK ISBN: 978-1-907992-82-7 • US ISBN: 978-1-907992-83-4 • £7.99/$9.99 CAN $12.99

It's where horrors come to be themselves, and the dead pause to rest between worlds. Recently widowed and unemployed, Richard Carter finds a new job, and a new life for him and his daughter Serena, as manager of the mysterious Deadfall Hotel. Jacob Ascher, the caretaker, is there to show Richard the ropes, and to tell him the many rules and traditions, but from the beginning, their new world haunts and transforms them. It's a terrible place. As the seasons pass, the supernatural and the sublime become a part of life, as routine as a morning cup of coffee, but it's not safe, by any means. Deadfall Hotel is where Richard and Serena will rebuild the life that was taken from them... if it doesn't kill them first.

 WWW.SOLARISBOOKS.COM

Follow us on Twitter! www.twitter.com/solarisbooks